Never Too Old for Romance

Other books written by Barbara J. Peters

The Gift of a Lifetime: Building a Marriage That Lasts
He Said, She Said, I Said - 7 Keys To Relationship Success

Never Too Old for Romance

Barbara J. Peters

To a long-time friend who showed me that romance
lives within every soul, young or old.

"For all sad words of tongue and pen, the saddest are these, 'It might have been.'"

~from *Maud Muller*, by John Greenleaf Whittier

Introduction and Acknowledgments

Writing this book was both a labor of love and a mission. The novel follows one woman's quest to rediscover herself in ways she had forgotten existed. My hope is that the story will be an inspiration for others to achieve romantic love and fulfillment. This book is about confidence, taking risks, and making good use all of the 1,440 minutes of each day.

I must thank my lifelong friend, Dana Lois Axel, who has known me since childhood. For all of our sixty-seven years as friends, we have been watching each other's life unfold. She contributed her expertise in astrology to provide another dimension to this tale. It is a gift to have her support and encouragement.

Dr. Ellen Logan, a colleague and friend, read each chapter as I brought them to the office. I appreciate her support, her English-teacher expertise, as well as her knowledge of romance novels, enabling me to stay on track. Finally, thanks goes to Dr. George Philip Popper, who listened avidly as I read chapters to him. He is responsible for the opening quotation from John Greenleaf Whittier.

While this account is fantasy, there are threads of reality throughout the pages, with all names, locations, and events changed sufficiently. The reality afforded me the chance to make the characters more believable. I hope that all readers, women and men, can find a positive, life-affirming way to see their golden years.

1

It was twilight. The irascible Florida sky, wide and threatening, promised anything from a cloudburst to a light wind. When Melanie Schulman got out of her white BMW convertible in the parking lot of the Boca Raton Hilton, a slight June breeze wrapped her knee-length dress around her, revealing a curvy figure. Although she was nearing sixty-six, she looked young and attractive, with hardly a wrinkle. She'd contemplated eye surgery, but as a nurse, she was scared of operative procedures and pain. When she was out with her thirty-eight-year-old daughter, people often mistook them as friends, which always made her feel good. So she thought: *To heck with the surgery! They'll have to love me, sags and bags.*

Men still did a double take from time to time. Although she was a brunette with long, stylish hair, she wore it with a few blonde streaks, much as she did in high school. Because she had a pretty face, with a turned-up nose and a smile that warmed the heart, Melanie still had the "wow" factor. But she was the only one who didn't realize this fact. It was as if she no longer saw herself as attractive.

Today, she and Lois Drazin (the best friend she grew up with) had a drink date. They were soul mates in every way. They still borrowed each other's clothes, and before they were married, they often double-dated. Even though they had been in different cliques in high school, they had remained friends. Lois was a sweetheart, always ready to help a friend.

Just as Melanie walked up to the curb, she spotted her friend getting out of her two-door sports Mercedes. Lois was a leggy blonde with an even Florida tan. The copper tone of her skin magnificently set off her green eyes. Although Lois loved haute couture, she shopped at Marshalls with a keen eye for knowing exactly what she wanted. She wore a 4.5-karat diamond ring and a wedding band, but somehow her ensemble still looked fashionably understated. She was unpretentious in her own way, and loved a night in with popcorn and a martial arts movie.

After a quick hug, they entered the white-marble lobby of the hotel. Melanie's earnest smile brightened her pretty face; but Lois, a discerning friend, could tell that something was on Melanie's mind.

They were still waiting for their drinks on the lanai by the pool when the setting sun sent a rainbow shimmering across the fountain spray arising from the center of the pool. It got their attention.

"Look at that," remarked Lois. "Means something big is about to happen."

Grinning, Melanie said, "That's either hopeful or foreboding."

Lois shared her grin. Both women were analytical. Lois's two grown sons lived out of state with their families, and she was retired, which gave her a lot of time to delve into astrology. She had been begging to do Melanie's astrological chart. While Melanie had no interest in astrology, she knew that Lois saw merit in it.

The drinks came, and the middle-aged waiter gave the two attractive ladies a big smile.

Lois, thoughtfully sipping her drink, said, "So what's bothering you? Is it the e-mail message from some guy we knew back in high school, coming out of the blue?"

"Well, yeah. You know how it is," Melanie said. "My personal life right now is far from ideal. I've been living a rather uninteresting life." Then suddenly out of context she added, "It's peculiar that I don't remember him at all."

Lois remarked, "From my recollection, he was a nice guy, kind of smart. In fact, he even wrote in my yearbook! My guess is that you're hoping that this goes somewhere beyond just a friendly chat?"

Blushing almost imperceptibly, Melanie leveled her gaze at her friend and said, "I'd be lying if I told you that it didn't get me thinking. About everything. Like I could fool you anyway. The reunion is next June, so I'll have a whole year before getting a good look at him."

Lois sipped her drink, her eyes full of interest. "You looked him up in the yearbook, of course."

Melanie grinned again. "Of course. He's quite handsome, if that's something to hang your hat on. I don't remember even talking to him. But who can remember? It's been so long ago. As you know, I was a cheerleader, and your friends and mine were as far apart as Alaska is from Australia. That much I remember."

Soon, the hors d'oeuvres arrived. Nibbling a mozzarella stick, Lois said, "You seem like you are flattered with his attention. The way you blush when you talk about him gives you away. Come on Mel, let me in."

"Okay, it's true," Melanie said. "I am getting a bit ahead of myself. But it all makes me wonder if it's too late. Why am I thinking like this? The die is cast. I already have a husband, who apparently could care less if I'm around. Do people our age make midlife changes and come away happy? Or do they just get new troubles in a different pair of pants?"

"Who knows?" said Lois. "Life is complicated and uncertain. We often don't get to know the outcomes. If you let me do your chart, I might be able to see some trends. One thing for sure, I can see this in your eyes: You're excited about the possibilities."

Instead of the expected mirth, Melanie lapsed solemn, a twinge of apprehension tempering her expression. "Is that a bad thing?" she asked seriously. "Perhaps I should forget all of this childish day dreaming and walk away from it."

Lois shook her head. "How many years have we known each other? I'm betting that you can't walk away. I know you too well. Your curiosity has a hold of you, and now it's too late."

Melanie wouldn't admit it to her friend, but her life was bland. She felt blessed with material goods, a worthwhile career, and terrific kids who were now grown. But was life supposed to be so dull at this age? She felt closed off. She was so starved for affection and love that any glimmer of excitement and male attention was bound to move her. She knew that Lois was right—she couldn't walk away.

***

Arriving home from her day at work, Melanie parked in the driveway of her sprawling ranch with a Spanish-tile roof. Out front there were transplanted coconut palms. Flowers of bright yellow and white led the way to the front door. She sat in the car, marveling for a few minutes before going in. She looked at the house and grounds. The lawn and shrubbery had just been cut, and the sweet smell of freshly cut grass was in the air.

What I always wanted: a beautiful home, a useful job, and ... The missing element! A life rich with passion, romance, and fulfillment. Well, maybe romance was a pipe dream, but at the very least, contentment should be in the picture.

She loved the house, and she had decorated it according to her personal taste. The colors were close to nature (ochre, green, beige, and earth tones), which enhanced the overall serenity and gave the feel of the outdoors.

The house was quiet as usual when she walked in. Her only welcome was from her dog, Schneider, an eight-year-old King Charles Cavalier, whose name she had lifted from one of her favorite soap operas of the sixties. He rocketed into Melanie's arms. Schneider made up in enthusiasm for what he lacked in size. He was small; his elegant, silky coat featured tri-colored markings. His face wore the perpetual frown of the breed, with soulful eyes and a sweet, "melting" expression.

Melanie spent time greeting him and easing his loneliness, smiling and laughing at his zealous antics. He was the apple of her eye, because her children had flown from the nest long ago and created their own families. "Are you that glad to see me, you old charmer, or are you just hungry?" she chuckled as she slipped off her shoes and looked around to see what needed to be cleaned. Quite frequently when she came home from work, she had to clean up a mess in the kitchen that her husband had left before dashing off to a golf date. This day was no different.

She understood his passion for golf. After all, she enjoyed tennis, a game that kept her heart healthy and her legs toned. But she did resent his foregoing a more intense personal relationship with her, in favor of golf.

With a sigh, Melanie went to the refrigerator to check out what there was for dinner. "Guess it's going to be leftovers again tonight," she told Schneider, who was busy with his own evening meal. She popped a dish of spaghetti and veal cutlet in the microwave, poured herself a small glass of wine, and as soon as the meal was ready, she took it to her computer in the den.

She was new to the technological age, having been led to it by her adult children, Edward (who was forty-one) and Meaghan (who was thirty-eight). Eddie had kidded her about being a "Luddite" because of her resistance. She had to look up the word before understanding that it referred to those people who resisted technological advances. But now, considering how lonely she had been feeling these days, she looked forward to being on the computer. Even though her job as a cardiac nurse was fulfilling, it still left her with a lot of time on her hands. To a great extent, she felt that over the last decade, that her life had narrowed, almost as if she were now painted into a corner.

Her fascination and interest in the Internet had a lot to do with pleasant anticipation. It piqued her imagination and led her into a larger dimension. It was fun to check e-mail and find messages from friends. Right now she was focusing on an upcoming fiftieth high school reunion, to be held next June. For Melanie, the Internet had its own special kind of expectation, allowing her to wander into another world. It provided her with a quiet hope that something interesting would be waiting for her. She looked forward to being online, because the Internet seemed to promise almost anything you were looking for. She was looking for friendship, hope, and interesting banter with friends. Whenever she sat down to the computer, the Internet stirred her with its possibility to provide what she was lacking in her life.

This day, her heart leapt at the notice of "You have mail." She quickly punched the appropriate keys, and there it was: a note from Mark.

Melanie,

I've been enjoying chatting with you. In case you don't remember what I look like, there are two photos on my somewhat-vestigial social media site. If you can't access them, let me know ... Never really got into all the social media technology, but thought it would be fun to see if any of our classmates were still around. It is interesting to reconnect with people from the past.

I did follow your link, by the way. Looks like life is treating you well. Happy to see it. By the way, is that a grandkid in your photo? So cute! How old is she?
  Regards,
  Mark

Melanie's jaw dropped in awe of Mark's pictures. Just like in the yearbook picture, he was still quite handsome, with blond hair and a mystery in his piercing blue eyes that promised something beyond merely good looks. She replied to the e-mail, answering the mundane questions first. Then she slyly suggested that they use personal e-mails for future correspondence; she was hoping for a more intimate conversation to develop. She wrote:

Mark,
  Please e-mail me directly. I usually don't check these social media sites very often, as I, too, am not a big fan. (She then provided a link to her e-mail.)
  Would love to hear more about you and your life.
  Yours,
  Mel

Two days later, she got an e-mail directly from Mark, which made her heart leap into her throat.

Melanie,
  So glad to have your personal e-mail. I might just be coming to your neck of the woods in a few weeks for a business trip. My career often causes me to travel. We can get into that later. It sure would be nice to meet you again, after all these years. What do you think?
  In the meantime, I'd like to hear more about your life, and I would be happy to acquaint you with mine. We do have a history in common, and we still probably know a lot of the same people.
  Regards,
  Mark

Melanie took a deep breath; her heart was pounding. He was coming to Florida? If he only knew! This was so exciting. Her imagination took off on flights of its own, over which she had little control. She quickly responded and agreed to correspond. She was so bold as to give out her phone number, just in case he had the urge to talk. Melanie felt like a schoolgirl again, and she was enjoying fantasies of the unknown. She felt as if she was being pulled to him with a magnet. Still unsure of his marital status, she decided to opt on the cautious side.

The next few days she had a twinkle in her eye as she went through her usual daily activities. She allowed herself to fantasize and take trips down memory lane.

As the days went by, the two became more than pen pals, asking each other questions about each other. They shared intimate details of their lives, getting to know each other better, laughing together and enjoying their talks. They got personal, seeming to connect on many levels. The topics they talked about had no censorship. It was as though the almost fifty years since school was a mere illusion.

E-mailing each other became the highlight of her days. She went to sleep thinking of him and woke up thinking of him. She was falling in love, and she told him so.

Then one day his phone call came, unexpectedly. That changed the dynamics of the relationship, bringing them even closer. Hearing his voice added another dimension to their growing connection.

During one of the phone calls, he revealed to her that he'd had a "crush" on her for a year and a half during high school. At the time, he hadn't asked her out because he didn't have a car, and he didn't think she would be interested in him. He said that he remembered sitting behind her in a class, and he called her a "goddess." He said he remembered her being funny and genuine, unlike the other girls in her crowd. She couldn't stop herself from wondering what would have happened if he had asked her out. But that was more than forty-five years ago, back in Brookline, Massachusetts, where they grew up. A lot of time had passed since they'd walked the same halls. Was it now too late for a second chance?

Melanie returned her thoughts to the present. She wondered, *What will I do if he asks me out?* She was unhappily married, but still married. Was the answer in the stars? Should she let Lois do her chart? Lois certainly believed it would be beneficial, and Melanie knew her friend would never be anything but genuinely honest with her. *My gosh!* she suddenly thought. *What if the chart reveals that Mark is supposed to be a big part of my life? What if my life still holds the promise of world travel and adventure, as well as romance?*

So many ifs! Ultimately what Melanie asked herself was, *Should I wait and let it happen, or should I find my own direction?* She knew there was a lot of cynicism about astrology and downright phoniness, too. But there was something alluring about the concept of letting the stars plot the future. Maybe she should do the chart, after all.

2

Melanie was finishing a hurried coffee in the break room when her beeper went off showing an emergency in the ER—possibly someone with a heart attack. She tossed down the rest of the coffee and was on her way. She hadn't had time for lunch. She sighed; it was another normal day at Boca Raton Regional Hospital. With the city's large elderly population, the hospital had no shortage of people with cardiac problems.

She often thought back on why she chose nursing as a profession. After her daughter was born, she got the inspiration to be a nurse. She started out wanting to work in the delivery room; but the cardiac unit, with its hint of destiny, claimed her soul. She never regretted the decision to leave babies for the chance to "mend a broken heart." Little did she realize that this metaphor might someday characterize what would happen to her own life.

Unlike other nursing jobs, cardiac nursing didn't involve mundane patient care and maintenance. Instead, every day she was part of someone's life and death drama, and she was right in the midst of the action. If what was happening that day wasn't an emergency, it was, at the least, interesting, emotional, and stressful. That work fit her nature. When her beeper went off in the break room, her seven-to-three shift had been almost over; but she knew now that she wouldn't be leaving until late afternoon. Often she was required to do double shifts, and she had worked her share of such shifts in the last year.

It was nearly six when she returned to her station from the ER, weary and limp. She observed a knot of nurses clustered around something on the station's counter. When they parted, she saw a floral arrangement. It was rather pretty, consisting of two light purple orchids growing in each other's shadow and appearing to reach out for one another, one a bit taller than the other. For a moment, it took her breath away. Nurse Grant said, "It's for you." Melanie noticed that her colleague had a little smirk.

The card read: "Couldn't resist the symbolism. Hope you like it. Mark."

Though surprised, she still had to veil her delight while answering general questions as well as inquisitive stares. She said, "Oh, it's from an old friend."

On the drive home, she kept thinking about the orchids and their artistic symbolism. She knew *she* hadn't mentioned their "symbolism"—but *he* had, so it wasn't as if she was giving the arrangement's romantic appearance more weight than it deserved.

She glanced over at the beautiful plant on the seat next to her. *Should I take it home? How will I explain it? But I'm not going to throw it away. Absolutely not!* Still, she hated to lie to her husband about it, so she struggled with the problem. Finally, she convinced herself that one little tiny white lie couldn't hurt. *I'll say it's from a grateful family of a patient I saved.* In fact, there had been occasions when she'd received gifts from patients or their families. It was against hospital rules for her to accept such gifts, but her husband probably didn't know that. *The hell with it. Lenny probably won't even notice the orchids anyway. These days he has little use for anything other than food and golf balls.*

When she got home, she saw that there was an e-mail from Mark.

Melanie,

Hope you liked the orchids. As I said, I couldn't resist the symbolism.
Sincerely,
Mark

She quickly dashed off a reply.

Mark,

Got the orchids, and loved them. I'm not very good at taking care of plants, but I will do my best with this one. It was so thoughtful of you; and yes, I do see a relationship between them. Wondering about your business trip. Any news? Thinking about meeting in person soon is really appealing. Please keep me informed.
Melanie

She knew that she was getting bold, but she felt a need to move ahead. There had been enough innuendo and guise. Though she didn't want to appear brazen or needy, she was anxious to get on with this romance, wherever it was going, if anywhere.

Mark responded to her note with a phone call. Taking a deep breath, she answered, "Hi, Mark. I wasn't sure it was you."

"Why?" he joked. "You have other suitors calling all the time?" There was merriment in his words, and she was glad about that.

"No, silly. Thanks again for the orchids. I love them."

"If the nurses on your job are anything like the secretaries here at my law office, you had to field some questions. Am I right?"

"Yes, you are. You never did tell me where you worked."

"I'm a partner in a law firm. We specialize in entertainment law, which is big out here in La La land."

"I never heard Los Angeles referred to in that way," she chuckled.

"Here in my business, that's what it's called."

"What exactly does your business do?" she asked.

"We are the legal reps for a whole host of celebrities. They range anywhere from an actor such as Kevin Bacon to a rock star such as Tom Petty."

"You actually know those people?"

"Intimately. After all, their lives and their futures are in our hands."

"So you live a glamorous life," she surmised.

"Sometimes," he agreed. "But often it's just boring lawyer stuff. It pays a lot, though, and the pay allows me some of the luxuries of life."

"Such as?" she asked, curious.

"A beautiful forty-foot yacht, travel to exotic places—pretty much whatever I want." Yet, there was a hint of sadness in his voice. "Frankly," he disclosed, "when you're not happy, life— everything, really—is kind of meaningless."

"I am so sorry, Mark," she said sympathetically. "I guess that answers my next question."

She didn't ask; he volunteered, saying, "I'll probably lose half of it in the divorce I'm planning, but I will still have enough for my lifestyle."

"Divorce? I know you said you were not happily married, but I didn't know the marriage was at that point. What's so bad that has made you think of divorce?"

"That's the hook: We *should* be happy. We have more than most, and I love what I do. I have enough money to indulge myself, and yet ..."

"Do you love her, Mark?"

He paused briefly, then said, "That's hard to answer. She is the mother of my kids, and my wife of over thirty years. I guess that is worth something. The sad part is that I am not 'in love' with her."

"That is too bad," was all that Melanie could think of to say. Then she asked, "What does she do?"

"Susan is an interior designer. She's talented and has clientele worldwide. At the moment, she's in Provence, in the south of France, designing a chateau for some rich New York gynecologist."

"Wow!"

"I know it sounds great, but how she handles her work is part of what is wrong with our supposedly perfect life. Susan obsesses about her craft and works at it night and day. She travels in a clique that includes her assistants and various girlfriend hangers-on. We rarely see each other."

"Don't you make plans to be together?"

"Sometimes. But our plans never work out; something always comes up. I mean *always,* which makes me believe that even if she had the time for us, she has little interest in me. We have been living parallel lives for the last ten years. It is getting rough on me."

"I'm sorry for you," Melanie said sincerely.

"Don't be. I'd be depressed if I thought you think of me as someone to be sorry for. I've been contemplating this divorce for a long time. But not wanting to hurt the kids has kept me from doing anything about it. My finding happiness didn't seem as important as the unhappiness I would cause others. The decision is difficult, to say the least."

She was about to say something when she heard Lenny's car in the driveway. She had not expected him to be coming home at this hour. Usually on poker nights with friends from his engineering firm, he arrived home late. Melanie had to think quickly about how to subtly end the phone call with Mark.

"Just a second, Mark," she said deftly. "I have another phone call. I have to get it."

She waited a few seconds and then got back to Mark. "I'm so sorry, this is something I have to deal with at work. Kind of an emergency. Can I have a rain check on our conversation?"

He agreed, and quickly she was off the phone. The wonderful romantic interlude abruptly ended, and she was back to the boring reality of her marital life. As usual, there was little normal chatter between Melanie and Lenny. He grumbled something about the game being cancelled, said he had grabbed some pizza out, and settled in front of the TV with a beer to watch *Monday Night Football*. She could see his paunch in silhouette, and the light played off his balding pate. *He had been attractive once,* she thought.

Melanie went to her room and lay down quietly on the bed. But her mind was a riot of thoughts. Hearing about Mark's life made her realize how much she wanted to do yet in her life. She felt utterly stuck, lonely, and bored, as if her horizons were limited. She wondered about her feelings for Lenny. She wasn't "in love" with him. It seemed ironic to her that she and Mark didn't have the love in their marriages that they wanted. Yet at the same time, they were talking to each other about falling in love. Her mind wandered back up North to where they went to school, to where things seemed simple, where there was a change of seasons, and where sometimes dreams come true.

She was anxious to continue her talks with Mark. She decided that she shouldn't shoot an e-mail off to him until the next day; doing it sooner would look too desperate. The last thing that she wanted for him to see was how much she was beginning to think she needed him.

3

The next day when she came home from work, Lenny's golf clubs were not in the front hall closet, so she knew he wouldn't be home for several hours. This time would be perfect to talk to Mark. As usual, her heart was thumping in her chest when Mark came on the line.

His voice was steady. She sometimes wondered if her voice made her sound like a love-struck schoolgirl. Did she talk too fast? Did she sound nervous? This excitement was such a drastic change in the course of her mundane life, that surely her inexperience must show.

She soon found their conversations getting easier, smoother, and more fun. Her inhibitions slowly melted. There were some crucial questions she had to ask soon, and she was looking for an easy way to ask these questions without being viewed as forward.

He kept bringing up memories that she had long forgotten, such as classes they had taken together, football games they had attended, and school trips. Melanie was usually part of whatever scene he was describing, but she had no recollection of the events. It was amazing how much he remembered after so many years, when in contrast, her own memory was a blur. She wondered, *Why can't I connect to these details?* In any case, it was incredibly flattering that he remembered her so well.

At some point in the conversation, the topic of how physical appearance changes over time came up.

"I hope you aren't expecting too much," he said honestly. "I am a lot older than your school day memories of me, whatever they are," he added with humility.

Melanie felt awkward talking about this subject. "And likewise," she managed to say. "Although I'm in good shape, and I don't really look my age, I'm not young anymore. I hope you are not disappointed. I carry a few extra pounds for my height, and I don't want you to think you will see the yearbook version. Don't anticipate too much."

Then he said something she hadn't expected. "Just to be with you will be all my heart can bear. The more we speak, the more I am enchanted by you."

She realized suddenly that it was a good thing he couldn't see her at that moment, because she felt a blush warm her cheeks. Was he just a romantic devil, or a terribly sincere man? She was not used to these kinds of compliments.

Eventually, Mark ended up talking about his wife. He told Melanie about some of Susan's shortcomings. His comments, oddly enough, provoked Melanie with envy. Melanie feared that she could not possibly be as interesting to Mark as Susan.

No matter what Susan's faults were, Susan lived a glamorous, exciting lifestyle. Clearly some of this lifestyle was business-related, drinking and partying with the glitterati in order to promote her interior design services. But Susan's drinking "on behalf of the business" wasn't the only thing that irked Mark about her personality. He had a list. For example, Mark insisted that Susan loved her adult children too much. Melanie wondered how anyone could love too much. *Isn't love too precious a commodity for one to lavish too much?*

Another of Susan's quirks, according to Mark, was her materialism. He used the term "bottomless pit" to describe her shopping sprees, her obsession with fancy, expensive cars (currently, her black Jag), and her over-whelming preoccupation with jewels, clothes, and furniture. There was no satisfying her lust for things, because there was always something better around the corner that she simply had to have. As far as that goes, Melanie rationalized, who doesn't like money and the things it buys? Because they could well afford it, why was he complaining? That she bought things didn't exactly seem like a deal breaker.

So despite Mark's list of Susan's faults, Melanie was still jealous of Susan. She wondered if Mark was jealous in any way of Lenny. She reviewed Lenny's faults with Mark, sparing only a few details. She saw Lenny as living in the faded glory of his youthful football exploits. He was the kind of a guy who never forgot the roar of the crowd from the bleachers; or perhaps in his mind, he was still hearing their adoration. At work and play, he was continuing to live for accolades. He wanted very much to shine. To this end, he worked hard to be appreciated. Having earned lots of money from his hard-charging style, he was generous with it, but controlling. Melanie had decided that it was better to rely on her own money, despite being married to a wealthy husband. She knew she could live with all of Lenny's faults except one: he had no interest in her romantically. The thrill of sharing their sexuality together had long since died. She felt abandoned and undesirable, yet still fully interested in love and affection.

She couldn't believe that she was telling Mark all of this. Discussing it with him was like a confession, as if she bared her soul. Even more startling was that Mark replied with equal candor, saying that the romance had completely evaporated in his marriage.

Would meeting change their lives? The promise was intriguing. Melanie's mind was racing as they discussed plans to rendezvous. She needed to think of a good excuse to be out of the house. Not that Lenny would care that much if she was missing for a while. As long as his dinner and other needs were taken care of, he might not even notice.

Before the call ended, Mark told her what days he would be in town and the name of the hotel where he would be staying. Melanie had a choice of days to see him, as Mark was going to be in town for five days. Was there to be more than one night? She picked her husband's card night—Tuesday.

By the weekend, she had cold feet. Where was her courage? She wanted to step back into the closet. Too many questions plagued her. Her obsessive thinking about the meeting was raising the hackles of her paranoia, and at times she was ready to back out. It was as if there could be no middle ground; if he wasn't absolutely positively bowled over by her, she would be unhappy. *Will he be disappointed in me? Or will he be thrilled? Is my body in good enough shape to share with a new man?* In the end, she realized that these questions would be answered fully only when she was alone with him.

When Lois called late one afternoon, she asked, "Getting nervous?"

Melanie sighed. "So nervous, I'm thinking about blowing it off."

"I wouldn't do that, girl. Listen, I took matters into my own hands, and I worked on your chart. Guess what?" Lois didn't wait for Melanie's reply. She blurted, "Uranus is transiting your seventh house!"

"Let me see … Seventh house. Is that about partner-ships?"

"Impressive!" Lois exclaimed. "We see a shift away from the self toward a partner." She paused and then added, "I don't know anybody who needs a partner as much as you."

Melanie wasn't sure that she liked the sound of that comment. "You make me sound so needy."

"No," Lois insisted. "I see that in uniting with someone, you become a more valuable member of the world."

"Ha," Melanie said, laughing at how pretentious that sounded.

Lois laughed, too. "Okay, so we're all more selfish than that. The heck with the 'valuable member of the world' part."

"I don't know, Lois," Melanie mused, becoming serious again. "So your advice is 'full steam ahead'?"

"In your case, yes. For the past few years, I've watched you live a lonely life, and it has hurt me. Possibly this man has a purpose for you; and if so, you need to follow it. Remember, my friend, you're the captain of your own ship."

On the one hand, Melanie thought, *that sounds good. Wonderful. Beautiful, even. On the other hand, what if my ship turns out to be the Titanic?*

4

Melanie's anxiety had reached a fever pitch. Tonight, she'd meet Mark. Although it was getting near the time she must leave, she had not fully decided what to wear. She went through her closet and already had tried on several dresses. She wanted to be sexy, but not obvious. In her effort, she found that understating her look—making sexy subtle—was not easy. Anybody could be obvious about dressing sexy, but she didn't want that look. In fact, obvious was the last image she wanted to project. Her dress was black and long, with a modest slit at the leg. It was enough to show some leg, but not up to the thigh. For hairstyle, she decided on a slight curl, which framed her face, with a blonde streak just where it was in high school. Her make-up and her accessories were low-key; just enough, she hoped.

All kinds of thoughts percolated in her mind. Before she had come to any conclusion on one thought, she was off on another.

One thing she had made perfectly clear to Mark was that she was not promising a sexual liaison. She was intent on playing that issue by ear and going where her heart led her. She hoped that maybe something would happen, but she wasn't sure how things would go or what she would—or wouldn't—do until the moment arrived.

It had been quite a while since she'd had sex. That had been with Lenny, and as usual, it was underwhelming. When she thought about it, sex with Lenny was lackluster not

21

because he was older and out of shape. It wasn't that at all. It was that it left her feeling less wanted, less loved, and less sexy than ever. So while she longed to be wanted and loved, she certainly didn't crave more sex with her husband. Whatever magic there may have once been, was now gone.

Of course, it hadn't always been like this. There had been a time (not so long ago, actually) when she thought that this second marriage with Lenny was exactly what she had needed. Lenny felt so, too, at first. Melanie felt that she had done her part to make it work. Sadly, he quickly lost interest in her. That was so typical of him, all into it at first, and then on to something else. Or maybe it was that he simply wouldn't put any effort into the romance part of their marriage. Whatever it was, for the last several years, Lenny had relegated her and their marriage to routine, putting no special effort, thought, or feeling into any aspect of their relationship, including intimacy.

"Intimacy. Ha!" Melanie snickered in the empty room. That was something her husband could never understand, even on his best day. For him, sex was just a physical thing. As long as he was satisfied, he considered it as a successful encounter.

Then her thoughts shifted to Mark. He had told Melanie that he hadn't had sex in years. The reasons were important; but for the moment, the point was that Mark must have a lot of sexual energy stored up. Melanie couldn't help but smile when she thought about that, not because she enjoyed his frustration, but because of the potential that it offered to her.

Yet she couldn't help wondering about a man who had not had sex in years. Wasn't that unnatural? Would such a sex-starved man try to pressure her, even if she wasn't ready for such a big step? All of these thoughts hurtled through her mind, each one bringing up concerns she had not considered seriously before. Up until now, this meeting had to do with fantasy and a kind of poetic, rather surreal love affair, full of passion and love. This romantic imagery didn't include the rather graphic act of sex itself.

If they did end up having sex, what would it be like? Would he be gentle and loving? From the sounds of his lack of a love life, he might be a raging bull. How would she know after all, for all intents and purposes, he was a stranger.

Another thought assailed her. What if we are lusting for sex because we are both deprived? Will love come in? Is mere sex good enough for me, without love?

She was absently twirling a lock of her curls when the phone rang. It was Lois.

"So," her friend said, rather succinctly.

"So?"

"Yeah. So what do you think? Are you going to go through with it? I know you well, Melanie, and I know how you vacillate about things."

"Of course. I'm getting ready now."

"I don't mean getting dressed," Lois said with a girlish giggle. "I mean getting undressed."

They shared some nervous laughter, but it served to make Melanie even more stressed out. "I don't know, Lois. I never promised him anything."

Lois said, "Of course not. But you know what you have in mind."

"No. I really don't. It's nice to think about. But what if we wind up having no interest in each other? What if there is no chemistry? No sparks?"

"What's the chance of that?"

"A lot, I think. We haven't seen each other in umpteen years. I didn't even know him back then. I don't think I said seven words to him in high school. Not only that, but he has a beautiful wife at home."

"With whom he hasn't slept in years," Lois scoffed. "Why think about that?"

"Why? I think about everything. It's all so darn confusing."

Melanie could "hear" Lois's frown even over the phone. "Don't ruin it before it even begins," Lois said. "After tonight, all your questions will be answered, and you'll know."

"Yeah," Melanie murmured, "that's kind of what I'm afraid of. Up until now, it's a nice fantasy. I'm not even sure I want to go through with it."

But Lois didn't want to hear it. Before she hung up, she said, "Don't be silly. Remember, believe in the stars. I read your chart, and this bodes well for you." So good luck, I'm hoping good things for you."

Melanie was super conscious getting dressed. She had done everything she could to make herself sensual and alluring. The fingernails, the hair, the body grooming, all done and meticulous. She even did a bikini wax, "just in case."

Melanie was sitting on the bed, thinking things over, when she heard the door open downstairs. She called, "Len? Is that you?"

He called back, "Yeah."

"Isn't this your card game night?" she asked nonchalantly.

"It is. I forgot something."

She hesitated, not wanting to go downstairs dressed to the nines. Before she knew it, he was in the bedroom, searching the dresser drawers. She cringed; he was going to notice. But he simply glanced at her as he found whatever he was looking for. He mumbled "See ya," and he left. She heard the big lout's car engine fade off into the distance.

He hadn't noticed. This fact firmed up her resolve to go through with the meeting. She grabbed her keys and headed for the door.

The drive went too fast for her. She would have preferred it took longer. By the time she got to the hotel, her heart was thumping. *That's good,* she thought. *I'm excited. And I think I have an idea that will help me more to get into the mood.*

In a stall in the ladies' room, she slipped off her panties, and with a wry smile, tucked them into her purse. *There. That feels nice and free. And so sexy.*

5

Melanie waited in the hotel lobby, so tense that she had to consciously calm and control her breathing. Her eyes remained firmly fixed on the front revolving door. He was due. This was the big moment of the big day that she had been dreaming of. But her self-doubts still plagued her. She wondered if this wasn't just a foolish and hopeless escapade of a woman who expected too much from romance. *Am I worried about making a fool of myself, or am I worried about being disappointed? Probably both!*

She took out her cell to check the time. Suddenly in the middle of her worries, she saw Mark. The phone slipped from her grasp and dropped to the floor. Whatever her expectations had been, she was thrilled to see him. But there was no time to really assess him, as she wrestled with a clutter of emotions while quickly scooping up her phone. Her knees were rubbery, and she could feel herself shaking.

Mark spotted her, smiled, and approached. He took her hand in his, and their eyes met for a brief but magical moment. She sensed by the light in his eyes that he liked what he saw. She had heard of instances where people dating online had provided photos that were years out of date. Not Mark. He was movie-star handsome: blond hair with a bit of silver, straight white teeth, and a California tan. He seemed about five foot eleven, had an average build, and was physically fit. Maybe it was her imagination, but all these factors blended into a knockout of a guy. He gently draped an arm around her shoulder. He was warm and comforting, as if there was a powerful connection already. It was not at all like they were strangers, though in essence they really were. They hugged, and she hoped that her pounding heart wouldn't betray her excitement.

He held her at arm's length in the ritual of appraisal, and she was sure that the warm mask on her face must be visible to him. *Will he think I'm way too enthusiastic for a first meeting?*

"You blow me away," Mark enthused. "You are more beautiful than I remember, a true goddess."

Melanie knew she was blushing even more now. Shrinking mentally under his roaming eyes, her tongue tangled in her mouth. For a moment, she couldn't speak. Too many emotions were competing for her mind. He solved her dilemma by taking the lead. "Let's find a quiet corner of that lounge over there and catch up," he said. Melanie loved the sound of this man's voice. He took her by the hand, and she followed. They located a quiet nook and sat side by side. As close as they sat, she was sure he knew that she didn't have any underwear on.

She hadn't rehearsed anything that she would say to him. Of course, one thing was for sure. She certainly didn't want to immediately start talking about her dullard of a husband and her lackluster life.

Mark again came to the rescue by asking her what she wanted to drink, followed by some more visual appraisal. He wasn't exactly staring, but he made no attempt to hide that his eyes were undoubtedly drawn to her.

Melanie managed to catch her breath and rediscover her tongue. "So, at least I guess you weren't too disappointed?" she asked. She thought a little humor might help to break the ice.

Mark smiled, and something about this simple gesture made Melanie feel safe.

"I think it must be obvious that I'm not disappointed at all. How about you?" he asked.

"No disappointment here, either. You have the same twinkling blue eyes I remember, I don't know how true the old adage is."

"Which one is that?" Mark asked.

"The one that says the eyes are the window to the soul. I've always found that to be true," Melanie replied. "You can tell a lot from a person's eyes. At least you can if you're insightful."

Melanie was glad that they didn't start off talking about high school, because they had not been close enough to share any real memories. In effect, they were strangers and should have been able to start out talking about almost anything. Yet it seemed that neither of them wanted to start with any kind of dating-scene small-talk, such as your favorite color, or your favorite dessert, or your astrological sign. She always felt that kind of silly stuff was an excuse to talk about *something*, not really an effort to discover the other person.

They sipped their drinks and sat, simply gazing at each other, which helped settle her down. During that time, they shared some pleasant chatter about the rigors of modern air travel and security. He was a calm person, and his tranquility helped steady her.

At one point, he said, "You know, I wondered for the longest time whether or not this made sense."

"*This?*" Melanie asked, curious.

Mark grinned. "Yeah, this trip back to yesteryear."

"Any particular reason why it might not make sense?" she pressed, suddenly intrigued by his genuine frankness.

He didn't hesitate with his answer. "Well, I always felt that if I went back to the past looking for some kind of satisfaction or to rediscover a beautiful memory, I'd run the risk of a big letdown."

She gazed into his blue eyes. "Maybe you're just being superstitious."

This time he thought about it for a moment, and then he said, "I know what you mean, but I'm not quite sure I would label it 'superstition.'"

"What would you call it?"

"I'd say it was more simply trying to avoid disappointment. I think that's universal—we all want to avoid being disappointed by something." He then added, "Or by someone."

All Melanie could say in reply was, "Yeah. That's true. I suppose that's why so many people depend on the advice of … the stars."

Mark raised an eyebrow. "Do you?"

"Never tried it. I'm not exactly sure why. Probably afraid to be disappointed in what the stars tell me." Right after saying it, she smiled in a knowing way

With query in his eyes, Mark asked, "What?"

Melanie decided that honesty was the best policy. She said, "I have a girlfriend who not only believes in it wholeheartedly, but who also practices it."

"Has she ever done your chart?" he asked.

"No, but she wants to."

He cocked his head. "And you?" He left the question hanging.

"I guess what I'm really thinking is that on some level, I want there to be a certain amount of mystery about the future. At the same time, of course, I also want to know what life holds in store for me."

Mark lapsed a bit solemn. "I know life isn't good to you right now."

She lowered her head. *God! I didn't want him to see my dissatisfaction with life. But I guess it is pretty much out on the table already.* She recalled that she had previously told him so many details of her personal life during their numerous intimate phone calls.

He took her hands in his and caressed them for a minute. Then he said, "What is your definition of love?"

She was as much shocked by the question as she was in awe of it. What Mark had asked her was deep, and she wasn't sure what to say. It wasn't because she hadn't thought deeply enough about it. The fact was, he was almost a stranger to her. Here she was, in a hotel, revealing highly personal beliefs, not just over the phone or the computer, but face to face! So she passed the buck and asked, "What is yours?"

She was curious to see his reaction, whether he would answer or slough off the question. But instead he said, "The best way I can define 'love' comes from a quotation from Dr. Wayne Dyer: 'Love is the ability and willingness to allow those that you care for to be what they choose for themselves without any insistence that they satisfy you.'"

Melanie was intrigued. Not quite sure how to respond, all she could think to ask was, "Is there anything else that you want to add?"

Mark said, "Yes. Love can't be measured. For example, one can't love more than another. It's an emotion different for everyone. Love exists in their internal world, not to be trivialized by absolutes or judged by another. When you love someone, you do it in your unique way. The feeling is spoken with your internal love language, often not stereotyped by the masses. Love is a difficult expression. It is more obvious by behaviors than words. Love is from the heart, and while most signals from the heart can be precisely measured to the millionth of a second or the tenth of a millimeter, love resists measurement. That's because love comes from one person and her or his psyche to another person."

All Melanie could do was to gaze longingly into his eyes. *Where has this guy been all my life!*

Mark said, "I know it seems surreal and incredible, but if I had a love from the heart, I would consider myself one lucky man."

No man had ever spoken so eloquently about love to her before. In one fell swoop, he had laid out his philosophy. What he had said was wise and sensitive. This combination was almost too good to be true. Could he be earnest about all of this, she wondered, or was it just some kind of line? She was quickly convinced of his sincerity.

What could she say back, she wondered, that would be equally as profound? Not only had she never considered the topic so philosophically, she'd also never spoken that freely on the subject to anyone. So instead of addressing the question, she managed to subtly shift the conversation by saying she'd be able to talk about it at dinner.

Melanie barely remembered dinner at the restaurant. She knew they'd had seafood. But what she remembered keenly was that she couldn't help keep her hand from drifting to Mark's knee and even his thigh as they conversed. Sitting side by side made it all too easy to touch him, and she took advantage of every minute. After dinner, they danced in the lounge, which was beyond wonderful. She felt as if she belonged in his arms.

They didn't do any type of fast dancing or high school swooning over each other, but as they swayed to the music, there was definitely a stirring—not only in the loins, but in the soul. She wondered how this intensity of feeling was possible with someone she had met merely hours before. Melanie's mind whirled.

How could I feel such wonderful passion? Was it all that time that I spent daydreaming about him? Is he feeling the same rush of excitement? I hope he is!

6

Before they knew it, the lounge was slowly emptying out to close. Melanie didn't want the night to ever end, yet she had to be realistic. What will happen if Mark asked her to stay? What would she tell Lenny? More lies. But she was drawn to Mark's every move, facial expression, and touch. *He is soft and so sensual!*

Yet she was scared, because staying the night with him just wasn't her style. After all, loveless or not, she was married. On top of that fact, she didn't want to give Mark the wrong impression. Back in school, they would call such a girl "fast."

But this is ridiculous. I'm a grown woman. As two consenting adults, why not?

There were no easy answers as they drifted into the hotel lobby, ostensibly to call it a night. Melanie wrestled with second thoughts as they settled into a quiet little nook near one of the windows. The secluded spot seemed like a world of their own. Something in Mark's eyes was calling her not to leave. He didn't say a word; but then again, he didn't have to.

Melanie knew that she couldn't let herself be ruled by her fear. She had to follow her heart. She could sense a life-changing moment unfolding before her eyes, faster than she could comprehend it. She wasn't in a hotel with just any man. Her intense emotions for him went past simple physical attraction.

His voice brought her back. "I sense a distraction, Melanie. Is anything wrong?"

Oh well, she was found out. "I was just wondering what we were going to do now," she said without guile.

He replied, "I hope you're thinking the same thing that I am."

Their eyes met as Melanie said, "I believe so."

"I want to spend the night with you. But probably you aren't prepared and need to go home," Mark said, ever the gentleman. "I understand. We didn't really know what would happen between us, did we?"

"Well, no. But I think we both had a pretty good idea. I want to stay with you tonight, but I can't figure out how." Reality barged in and took away from the magic of the moment. It was not so much that she was torn between right and wrong. If she couldn't manage this night away from Lenny, she'd have to go home. On the other hand, if she went home now, when she wanted Mark so badly, she'd be utterly disappointed. Melanie, usually a pragmatist, struggled with letting her emotions take the lead.

They sat close. His hands navigated her body, and he wrapped her in his aura. They were alone, and the rest of the world seemed to be so quiet that only their quick breaths were audible. He electrified her. Her nerve endings tingled sharply.

How had they moved to the elevator? "I am claustrophobic of elevators," she confessed.

"Oh, we can take care of that," Mark said. He held her close, kissing her intensely. Melanie swooned, weak with a passion that had lain dormant in her for years. She suddenly sprang to life and kissed him back deeply.

Arriving on the eighth floor, he escorted her to Room 807. She saw an enormous, king-sized bed. Beyond it, the curtains were open, revealing a spacious balcony.

"Let's have a nightcap outside," Mark suggested.

Melanie nodded. She rolled open the balcony door and stepped outside, waiting for him to prepare the drinks. She leaned over the railing, looked out at the lights of the city, and listened to the distant whoosh of the ocean surf. It was a soft Florida night. The palm fronds on the balcony whispered in the balmy breeze.

I can't believe I'm here. How far should I take this? This moment is too perfect.

When he came up behind her, she heard a barely audible "clink" as he set the drinks on a small glass table and slipped his arms around her waist. He snuggled his face into her hair and she had to catch her breath.

His voice was soft, yet powerful. "Your hair. It's so fragrant. It smells like sunshine and orange blossom." He nibbled on her ear lobes and ran his lips gently over her neck and cheek. She became highly aroused.

They gazed out into the night and enjoyed the nightcap. For the moment, they were both lost in their own thoughts. When he put his drink down, his hands wandered to her hips, paused, and felt only her skin beneath the material. He turned her around to face him.

"You had the same feelings as me?" He leaned her back to better look into her eyes.

She said playfully, "What were those?"

"The two of us together." He studied her face, his eyes roaming, appreciating, and feasting. When he kissed her, she left planet Earth and entered a new universe, one of soft, wet, probing tongues and a bliss so pure it left her breathless. Somehow all of this led to their ending up in the spacious bathroom, the door to the balcony still wide open.

As he removed her black dress, he suggested, "Let's get in the shower."

Mortified, she hastily arranged a towel over her body. She knew that he was seeing not an eighteen-year-old goddess, but a sixty-five year old. Yet she saw a delight in Mark's widening eyes that removed all her doubts. She threw caution to the wind, lowered the towel, and he lustily appraised her with the utmost approval. He wrapped his strong arms around her and began slowly kissing her neck as his hands explored her lovely curves.

Melanie felt her whole body come alive as she stepped into the hot, steamy shower. Getting in right behind her, he maneuvered his large hands around her, softly caressing her body with a bar of lilac soap. He let his hands slide and linger over her breasts, paying particular attention to her taut nipples. "That feels great," she purred as Mark expertly lathered her. She quivered.

"It gets even better," he whispered into her ear as his hand smoothly glided down her thigh and then tantalizingly, slowly made its way up again, touching and teasing just the right spot between her legs.

Although extremely vulnerable, she wanted to be his.

When they stepped out of the shower, he patted her down with a towel and then wrapped another one around her, just so.

She got into bed. Her next conscious thought was when she snuggled the sheet up over her breasts. He was standing next to the bed. He smiled down at her and pulled the sheet back to look at her, naked. She closed her eyes and waited for his voice.

He said, "You are stunning."

He was about to say more, but she reached up and drew him down to her, covering his lips with her own hungry kiss. If she had ever thought about being demure or in control, she forgot it. Her hunger was voracious as she let her body and soul be carried away to paradise. It was not hard for her to hold on tight as he moved over her with his strong, masculine aura and his demanding body. He fully navigated her well-endowed form, passing his lips lightly over her stomach, breasts, neck, up to her lips. Her skin exploded with sensations that had been in hibernation for years.

"You feel so good," he kept whispering in her ear.

"I want you," Melanie somehow managed to reply, her heart beating a mile a minute.

There was no discomfort when he began his intense yet gentle lovemaking. After all, it had been a long time since she had been intimate with her husband. But she need not have worried about her performance. Trembling with emotion and wrought with desire, she was moist in anticipation.

Both their needs were great. He drove to his climax, which was shattering and left him gasping for breath. After a few moments to recover, he was incredibly patient, gentle, and attentive to her needs. He softly touched her, discovering her important places. Her hoarse gasps of delight filled the room. Mark caressed Melanie until she, too, quivered in a pent-up release of physical need and passion. She lay motionless, her leg wrapped around him, and his arm around her. No one spoke for a while.

A soft breeze riffled her hair from the open patio door. She wanted to lose herself forever in this marvelous man. *Had two people ever wanted each other so much?* Her worries about her age disappeared. Melanie reveled in the moment. *I know I will remember tonight forever.* Like women the world over, for time immemorial, she wondered what he was thinking.

What have I done? Now what? Get up and leave? She had lapsed again into the real world, and she wasn't liking it a bit.

Finally he said, "I wish I were young again."

The remark caught her by surprise. With a wry grin, she lay on her side. She propped her head up on her elbow and asked, "Why? It doesn't seem that you're lacking anything."

"Well for instance," he pointed out speculatively, "we could make beautiful babies."

She laughed in pleasure.

"And if I were younger," he continued, "I would have more stamina. You're so breathtaking, I want to make love to you all night."

"I guess I am amazed we did what we did," Melanie said, looking around the room at scattered clothes, shoes, towels, and sheets. "Who knew we could feel and act like teenagers, sneaking behind closed doors in our parents' house, and hoping we won't be caught with our pants down."

He smiled and lapsed quiet, and she didn't interrupt the moment by saying anything. But when her curiosity got the best of her, she said, "Penny for your thoughts?"

"You'd need a lot of them. Like thousands," he gestured widely.

She smiled and said, "I'll bet my thoughts are worth even more."

He spooned himself into her from behind and snuggled, his whole body nestled into her every curve. They were like that for a while until she could feel him stirring. "Well, what do you know," he said, "I'm younger than I thought I was. At least with you."

This time lasted much longer. Things went easier and with much more exploring. He devoted lingering and thoughtful attention to her breasts, her nipples now fully aroused. He seemed fascinated with how pert they were. Mesmerized, he gazed at her, his face rapturous. She nibbled his earlobes and ran her tongue down his neck. He shivered with ecstasy. She said, "I think I now know every one of your sweet spots."

He murmured, "You can say that again."

Burying her lips in his hair, she whispered in his ear, "I can't get enough of you."

Mark was careful as he straddled her, mindful of maneuvering into just the right position to where the sensations were exquisite for both of them. His style of lovemaking was unlike anything she'd ever experienced before. He moved unhurried and deliberate, focused entirely on her pleasure. Melanie let her hands fall back over her head against the pillow. She closed her eyes and let him take her away to a far-off place. Surrendering herself to him like this, she felt completely free for the first time in a long time— maybe for the first time ever.

As his fervor grew and he slowly increased his pace, Melanie's mind was awash with thoughts and feelings too complex to process. The pleasure was so intense that it was blinding her to every other consideration. She grabbed his back tightly with her recently manicured fingernails. Her grip was not enough to hurt him, but firm enough to pull them even closer together, so that he was clear about what she wanted. Her hips rose up to meet his every thrust with a rhythm that seemed attuned to the most beautiful music in the world. All the while he would kiss her neck here and there. Then he would move back to her mouth with passionate kisses that sent her over the edge in a tidal wave of pleasure and blessed relief.

Both Mark and Melanie desperately wished it could go on forever. When another climax approached for Mark, it arrived with the intensity born of ardor and not need. He muttered, "Oh, Melanie! You're so damned beautiful."

She was exhausted but in a peaceful way, experiencing the familiar "orgasmic afterglow" that she had sadly thought she might never feel again.

The night had gotten late, and she should leave. Maybe she should call Lenny and tell him that her car broke down, so that she could stay. Perhaps she could tell Lenny that she'd had one too many to drive, so a friend offered her a bed until the morning. All sorts of ideas were circulating in her mind, and she had to do something. The truth was, she didn't feel like talking to Lenny, and Mark had fallen asleep. Perhaps she should go home, but she didn't want to. She wanted every minute she could get with Mark.

In the end, she texted Lenny with a phony story about staying at a friend's house after having a little too much wine. A few minutes later she received Lenny's one-word text reply: "Okay."

Melanie got up, closed the balcony door, and then went back to bed next to Mark, with too many thoughts racing through her mind to fall asleep quickly. She eventually did, but only for about an hour, waking up in the middle of the night. Slipping on his robe, she moved quietly so as not to wake him. She padded over to the small hotel fridge and got herself a little bottle of Chardonnay and a bag of peanuts. She heard him say, "Could you get me something cold?"

She looked over her shoulder. "What would you like?"

"Do they have beer?"

"Yes."

"Good."

Back in bed, she said, "If I'd known you were awake, I would have asked you."

He sipped the cold beer and sighed in appreciation. "I know you would have." He sipped again. "Ah, that feels so good. I was feeling parched."

Melanie winked at him and said, "I wonder why?"

He smiled. "Some gorgeous lady seems to have drained me."

After a nervous giggle from her, she said, "I'm not much of a beer drinker."

Mark said, "That's true of most women. But remember it's a German lager, very special."

"Everyone's different," she said. "If beer is special to you, so be it."

"I collect beer like some people collect fine wine. I've studied beer and its manufacture," he told her.

She sat up in bed and chuckled. "A beer connoisseur?"

"That's right," he grinned.

'You never mentioned it in your e-mails."

"Can't put a lifetime of quirks, idiosyncrasies, and preferences into an e-mail."

Melanie wondered—no, worried—that she had said something naïve. She didn't know if he was being serious or lighthearted, and she must have frowned.

When he laughed, she gazed intently at him. He said, "Don't look so serious. Of course we don't know everything about each other. At least not yet."

"I didn't know I looked serious."

He was gazing at her again. Although she liked it, she was now feeling a bit self-conscious. He said, "Don't worry."

"About what?"

"About whatever you're worrying about."

"What makes you think I'm worrying?"

"That cute little wrinkle at the corner of your eye."

"Wrinkle?"

"Yes," he said. "It seems to appear when you get serious. Also something that didn't show up in e-mail," he laughed.

"Sounds like you've studied me," she said.

"I have," he nodded with mock gravity.

"How's it going so far?" she asked.

He grinned. "Don't go fishing for compliments. You don't have to. In fact, I'm the one beginning to feel a certain lack of confidence. You're so damned gorgeous."

She ignored the last remark but said, "Lack of confidence? It sure didn't seem that way to me earlier."

He smiled. "I guess you inspired me."

She said, "I suppose I should be flattered. But do you know something?"

"What?" he asked, gazing at her again.

She liked this pillow banter. Or maybe it was the way they were talking. It sounded and felt like they had achieved an intimacy beyond the physical. "What?" he repeated.

She said, "I don't want to talk about things like that, because it reminds me that you had a life before me."

"And I didn't? You didn't?"

"No, it's not that. I mean, I'd like to think of us as exclusive, special. I don't want what we did with others to intrude on our time together."

They got quiet again.

Then she said, "Does that sound silly?"

"No. I know exactly how you feel. I don't want to share anything about you with anyone. That probably sounds immature and naïve, but that's how I feel."

She snuggled closer. The air-conditioning hummed quietly somewhere on the periphery of her consciousness. This night was either the start of a momentous time of her life, or something else. Not wanting to think about it, she cuddled closer until sleep finally overcame her in the pre-dawn hours.

7

Breakfast was surreal. Mark and Melanie picked at their food, their eyes locked on one another's. Something in their lives had ended, and something new was about to begin.

Melanie suspected that Mark was as puzzled and confused as she was. They had just made beautiful love and neither wanted to return to reality. They were so content, even in this bewildering state. The night's encounter still vivid, she relived it in her mind. She experienced the same tingly feeling. *Was it was ever going to happen again? She sure hoped it would.*

There were a few facts to face. First, they lived halfway across the country from each other. Second, they both had careers. Third, they were married to other people.

Mark had been thoughtful enough to run down to the hotel store and get her a toothbrush, toothpaste, and other toiletries to make her comfortable. Without speaking much, they got dressed and then took the elevator to the lobby. Melanie smiled timidly at other passengers. *What if I see someone I know? Even these strangers—do they know what I did?*

At her car, he kissed her goodbye, his lips clinging, and his eyes questioning. She drove away, her mind still somewhere else, her conscious self guiding the car home.

A few minutes later, her cell phone chirped. It chirped three or four times before she had the presence of mind to pull over and answer it. It was Mark. "Are you okay?" his voice trembled.

Should she tell him? She was more in love than she had thought possible. She wanted to marry him and be with him forever. Would he think she was crazy? Or would he feel the same? Still in the throes and insecurity of newfound love, she didn't want to speculate on his feelings, but she did so anyway. Having taken the risk, she now had to face the consequences. How could she be sure he felt the same? What could be worse than a one-sided love affair? Was he in it for sex alone, a fling on a trip away from home? She dreaded that thought. She had reached a plateau of life that was brand new to her, and she hoped she had not reached it alone.

So his call took her by surprise. She was not firm in her response, but holding back the tears, she said to him, "It's all so new and challenging. Let's talk later, okay?"

"Melanie, I want you. Last night was wonderful. Please don't go where I think you are going with your feelings. Don't make assumptions about us. I may completely shock you when you find out more of what I am about."

"I'll try, Mark," she replied.

He seemed unsatisfied and said, "Well, okay. Just know I will be thinking of you. Until I call again, goodbye."

She marveled at his perception. He realized she would be second-guessing everything. *I just shared all of me with a man I barely know. But he sure does know me. Damn!*

The rest of the drive home, she delved into introspection. On one hand, she felt wonderful and omnipotent. Her heart was soaring. *He'll be thinking about me.* And yet, she thought, *So what? What good does that do me?* What she wanted to do was get lost in him, dwell in the romance, and focus only on him. Instead, the first thing she planned to do when she got home was to run into the shower and wash away his scent and her guilty feelings.

Lenny met her in the driveway. She took a deep breath, because she wasn't practiced at deception.

With a wry grin, he said, "Are you sober now?"

With no matching mirth, Melanie replied, "Of course. Sorry I acted like an adolescent last night. It won't happen again."

He offered merely a dismissive wave and a lackadaisical, "See ya later." Not even a perfunctory kiss.

She was relieved that he was off to his hobbies as usual.

After a hearty and sincere greeting by a bounding, prancing Schneider, who had truly missed her, she headed for the shower.

As the hot water pounded her, she attempted to cleanse away her self-doubt. Her racing mind threatened to outpace her racing heart. By the very act of being in the shower, she couldn't help but crave Mark. *Will I ever see him again?*

But she could not relax. *I need to get a hold of myself. Tomorrow is a work day, and I am going to have to be on my toes. Lives, as usual, will be at stake.*

She called Lois and avoided her friend's only half-joking pleas for juicy details. Instead, Melanie insisted on making a date to find more about her stars. Was the answer there?

"What the heck?" she conceded to Lois. "What do I have to lose?"

8

Mark sipped his martini and gazed out the window of first class. He was deep in thought and barely noticed the patchy cumulus whipping by on his way to LA.

Did last night actually happen? Is it for the good? Should I make changes in my life? Or is it too soon?

He stretched his legs and loosened his tie.

"Is everything fine, sir?" At first he didn't hear the flight attendant. She asked again, "Sir? You okay?"

He looked up, his face blank. "What?"

"You need anything?"

"Oh, no. Nothing." Before she left, he added wistfully, "What I need, I left behind."

She smiled.

Whatever other doubts he had about what he was doing, there was no doubt that he missed Melanie already. Or was that emotion, too, just a flight into fantasy, based on the idealism of youth? After all, why hadn't he taken up with a woman from some other part of his life? Why high school?

His frame of mind easily segued into a look at his present life. He thought about his kids. Although they were grown, he would always think of them as his "kids." He considered his and Susan's successful careers and the luxuries that success afforded. He realized how all that money helped divert his attention from ever adequately addressing the many problems in the marriage.

He considered all the "ifs." If Susan had still been interested in sex with him, would he have betrayed her with Melanie? If Susan traveled less, shared some common interests with him, and been attentive, would he be happier with what he had? For years they had lived parallel lives, coming together solely for family functions and holidays, acting in front of all as if they were the happy couple. Who would have a clue as to the disconnect he felt?

So was he just looking for "variety," like so many other men his age? Mark had been raised with strong Jewish morals and values, had been bar mitzvahed, and had attended Hebrew School. All his life, he had done things the right way. His parents couldn't have expected more from him. But should he expect more from himself? He considered that perhaps his marriage wasn't dead, just sick.

As he continued such meandering thoughts, he realized that he preferred Melanie to Susan. This realization provoked deeper thought.

Do I prefer Melanie just because Melanie is new? Will it eventually be the same with Melanie as with Susan?

The answers weren't coming. But he reveled in the reality of the beautiful, near-mystical interlude. He didn't want to forget it. He didn't want things to get back to "normal" with his life. Mark was no longer in love with Susan. He didn't see love coming back without a lot of difficult counseling, something he was not interested in doing. He was unwilling to settle for the same old misery. His marriage had lost its meaning and promised no future. At best, remaining married was an accommodation with comfort and familiarity.

His wandering mind took him back to high school. Why hadn't he asked her out? All he could remember was that she was out of his league. He remembered Mrs. Gomez's Spanish class. He sat at the rear of the class, and Melanie sat in front. He recalled her brunette hair with the "blonde streak" down one side. How he loved the look of her, like a Victorian bisque doll.

A success-oriented kid, he had buried himself in his studies. It was the prudent thing to do. He wasn't very popular with the girls. A super-achiever, he was smart and skipped ahead one year. He wasn't as old as the kids in that grade, so he didn't drive a car when most of the other boys did. No girl wanted to go on a date with a kid who still rode a bicycle. He especially believed that about Melanie, because she was always with some "older" boy who drove a cool car. How could he measure up? So he just admired her from afar for a year and a half.

In a way, last night was a dream come true. Melanie was interested in him! But now there were all kinds of complications that involved a whole host of people.

By the time his flight was over the Rockies, he had made at least one decision: He would ask Susan for a divorce. Being a sensitive man, he rationalized that Susan would be happier, too. To make the divorce easy, he would offer her everything. After all, if it weren't for the kids, they would share very little. Certainly divorce would be a more noble option than simply running out and having an affair.

After Mark's second martini and a lavish lunch, he dozed off, pleasant dreams awaiting him.

Back in Boca Raton, Melanie, too, was struggling with an implacable dilemma. She didn't want to tarnish her wonderful memories of last night with feelings of guilt about her cheating. On the other hand, she knew that is exactly what she had done.

Still, the ecstasy was real. It lingered within her like a still-glowing ember. She still felt his essence. *Did I do the wrong thing?* She had thought that her days as a sexually active woman were long over. She typically wore simple clothes and little make-up. She did not indulge in the spa rituals of younger women who get periodic bikini waxes, weekly manicures and pedicures, to say nothing of facials and body massages. This was not the world she lived in. She stuck to nursing uniforms, baggy jeans, and shorts. Thong underwear, never! To the beach or pool, she wore a one-piece bathing suit. But Mark made her feel sexy and beautiful. She wanted to go buy some new clothes and visit the spa.

It was as if he had been in her life forever. She knew that they shared a history together, even if she couldn't remember him. When she thought of her hometown, she thought of the same neighborhood that he did: Benham's greenhouse on Brookline Avenue, Rede's Variety Store on Mill. The football games. Temple Sinai, where they went on the Jewish holidays. She and Mark had walked the same streets in those light-hearted high school days. She remembered stopping at the corner drugstore after school for a cherry soda and a bag of chips, gossiping with her girlfriends about boys, clothes, and the coming prom. So although she and Mark had never dated, they shared memories of growing up in that town. These memories were indelible, very much a part of them both.

It took her until late afternoon to arrange a drink date with Lois, who was eager to hear the details and so readily agreed to a six o'clock meeting at the Hilton, their usual meeting place. It was geographically convenient for both of them, and they liked the peaceful environment.

They ordered their usual cocktails.

"Well?" Lois burst out.

Melanie rolled her eyes. "Don't make me regret this. You look like you expect too much."

Still unable to suppress her eagerness, Lois blurted out, "For cripes sakes, just tell me what happened. What was he like? I've been fantasizing about this."

"He was everything I could hope for and then some."

"Did he look the same?"

Melanie grinned. "I had no trouble recognizing him from the picture he sent me over the computer."

"Did he recognize you?"

She grinned wider. "I'll say."

They talked about the date, even as Melanie scrupulously avoided the sexy parts. Finally, Lois declared, "For God's sakes, Mel, did you do it or not?"

Melanie lowered her head. She wanted to gloat about it, even as she realized how childish that was. But she couldn't help herself. "It was wonderful," she said, her eyes dancing with joy.

The tears came as soon as she said it. Lois reached over and took her hand. "Uh oh. I knew that this would happen. You're having doubts?"

"No. I'm happy, but so confused and so out of synch with my everyday life."

"I thought you'd feel this way," Lois nodded knowingly. "I suspected it wasn't going to be easy. Well I'm here. Let it all out."

"I feel so silly, crying on your shoulder about something I was going to do no matter what! I was able, willing, and ready. And now that I've gone and done it, I'm more confused than ever." She fiddled with her cocktail napkin.

Lois squinted as if she didn't understand yet, so Melanie continued.

"What I mean is, when he doesn't call again, I'll have to process the hurt. I quickly gave myself away to this man without looking at the consequences. Maybe I don't have the proper boundaries. Or perhaps I feel so deprived of love, that I lost my better judgment."

Lois lapsed quiet for a moment, then said, "I've known you for a long time, Melanie. We grew up together. We lived right behind each other, borrowed each other's clothes, and stood up for each other. Remember when I had to have my date, Richard, pick me up at your house, because my parents didn't want me to date a non-Jewish boy? What would I have done without you?"

Melanie laughed as she fondly recalled the memory. "Yes, how could I forget that one. We really did some crazy things in high school. I always wondered why we were never in each other's classes. But we stayed friends even though we ran in different crowds." Melanie grasped Lois's hand. "You have always been like the sister I never had. How lucky we were to have ended up near each other in South Florida. We do have a lot of history together, don't we? I'm fortunate to have you as a friend, Lois."

"So you really have fallen for him already, huh?" Before Melanie could answer, Lois continued, "I wanted to wait until now to tell you …"

Melanie raised an eyebrow. "Tell me what?"

"I did your chart," Lois revealed.

Melanie leaned forward, her eyes wide, and she grew thoughtful. "First, let me tell you that I have confidence in whatever you are going to tell me. And it's not because I am looking for something good. It's because I feel so close to you. I believe you could be nothing but honest and straightforward with me." She hesitated as they locked eyes. "And what did you learn?"

"Well, don't go thinking that your chart gives you all the answers," Lois advised. "Sometimes the chart can do no more than give you an idea that something is in the air."

Melanie looked up from her drink. "You don't have to worry about providing a disclaimer. Just tell me. Is there something in the air?"

Sounding very certain of her words, Lois said, "The chart says that Mark has a definite purpose in your life. At the moment, I don't know what that purpose is. The purpose will unfold as this relationship continues." Lois stopped talking, then she asked, "It *is* going to continue, isn't it?"

"The way I feel right now, I don't see how it cannot help but go forward. But I don't know what he is thinking."

"Well the stars are aligned to tell you this," Lois said, pausing to finish her drink. "He is going to have a great impact on your life, and that impact will change parts of you. Forever," she stressed.

Melanie's eyes grew wide. "Wow. So if I was thinking that I should consider this a magnificent interlude, I guess I shouldn't?"

"Uranus is transiting your seventh house. Uranus is all about change, and the seventh house is relationships," Lois said assuredly.

Melanie looked askance and wistfully murmured, "According to the stars."

9

Mark's plane descended through a thin layer of smog and approached LAX. The landing—a chirp of rubber and a thump, followed by the roar of reverse-thrusting engines—broke his reverie. Touchdown caused his stomach to be thrown into turmoil as he worried about what to say when he got home, and how to say it.

After retrieving his luggage, he walked outside the terminal and squinted in the bright sunlight. He stood on the curb and hailed a taxi. He told the driver his address and they began the twenty-five-minute drive to his home in Palos Verde Estates on the south shore. Looking out the taxi window at the familiar surroundings, he suddenly, uncharacteristically, found himself wondering what Susan's schedule was and whether she was home. He hoped she was. He needed to talk.

Before long, the taxi entered an area of cliff-top oceanfront estates in the exclusive community where Mark and Susan lived. The taxi pulled up to their home near Bluff Cove, just south of Haggerty's Beach. The white Mediterranean beauty sat regally atop a cliff at Ocean Front Estate. It had orange Spanish tile roofing and was so ensconced in meticulously manicured shrubbery that the greenery veiled its size. From the front lawn, Mark and Susan had sweeping vistas of the Pacific all the way to Catalina. He often sailed his forty-foot Atlantis cabin cruiser to the island, where he would anchor in the harbor at Avalon for the weekend.

When he went inside the house, it was quiet. His eyes swept the open expanse of the first floor, looking for Susan, knowing full well that she could be on the other side of the world. The place was wide open and spacious. The kitchen had a gourmet center island and overlooked a family room. He glimpsed inside the entertainment room, at its huge wet bar and wine cellar. Likewise, the office was empty, with its built-in cherry-wood furnishing plus multiple rooms for entertaining. He strode to the top of the winding staircase and looked in vain in each of the six bedrooms and their huge master suite; nor was she in the second-floor media room with wet bar.

He went back down through the first floor, past walls covered in modern art and sculptures teetering on strategically placed pedestals. Because of the open floor plan and the statuary, the home, in some ways, resembled a Roman villa.

Mark sighed and wandered outside to the terrace, where he gazed at the crystal aqua water in the kidney-shaped pool and attached spa. Imported coconut palms abounded, shading the poolside. To the side was the tennis court. Directly back was a panoramic summer view of the Pacific, now choppy in the afternoon, with the sound of the eternal surf a continuous whoosh.

He started thinking about his assets: the forty-foot Atlantis, the *Susan B,* docked at the local yacht club; his membership at the lavish Palos Verdes Golf Club; the rustic cabin in the Sierras; the two BMWs in the garage; the million-dollar piano from Liberace's estate, and much more. He considered his lifestyle: the vacations to Cabo and Acapulco in Mexico, fall trips to Europe, the safari in East Africa. Most men would be happy with all this and a beautiful, successful wife to boot. Then again, what good was any of that in a marriage devoid of passion?

He went back in to check the refrigerator and found a note from her on the kitchen table advising that she'd be home later that evening.

Actually, he thought, *that was better.* He breathed a sigh of relief, at least for the moment. She'd arrive in the early evening, which gave him more time to think about what he wanted to say. At this point, he wasn't sure what he even wanted, let alone how to say it. What he wanted to say was overshadowed by his memory of Melanie, her exquisite green eyes, the blonde streak in her hair. But he had to admit that her strong passion for him was what made him feel special. Finally, he felt alive and looking forward to life.

The strict Jewish culture he was brought up in left no room for immorality. He could only imagine what his beloved late mother would be thinking of him! However he felt that in retrospect, all that strictness was impractical, and those rules didn't really reflect life as most people had to live it.

On second thought he wondered, *Isn't that what all cheaters and dishonest people say?* He never wanted to think of himself in those terms, and it felt demeaning to even contemplate ascribing such labels to himself.

The truth was, though, that despite his wealth, he was not happy. Desperately, he wanted a life with Melanie. But perhaps such happiness was all a fantasy, a dream in which a mature man had no business indulging. After all, wasn't romance the stuff of youth? Was he kidding himself? He knew it was wrong to cheat, and that wasn't his plan—either for the short term or the long run. He had just been swept away by the intensity of it all.

If he were a more simple man, it wouldn't be so complicated. He wanted Melanie, evidently she wanted him, and that should be that. But he had many more considerations, which were all developed and honed from his strict ethnic upbringing, not to mention his own internal moral compass. His conscience was finely tuned, and he could feel it pulling him in multiple directions.

He spent the remainder of the sunny afternoon outside on his favorite deck chair, with his feet propped up on the railing. He gazed out at the churning Pacific, thinking.

When Susan arrived home early that evening, Mark met her at the door. She was smiling as she always did when he returned from one of his trips. She said, "How was your trip?"

He smiled back. "Good, good. Shall we dine in or out tonight? We have a lot to catch up on, and I was thinking going out would be easier."

"Okay, going out it is."

Will I have the courage to ask her for a divorce? he wondered. *After all, as flat as their marriage had been in recent years, they had never so much as mentioned divorce before.*

The La Venta Inn, with its ocean views, was one of their favorite eating places. The menu featured Cal/Med dishes; the barbecued calamari was Mark's favorite, while Susan rarely had more than a salad with fish or chicken. While they waited for their drinks, they gazed at the sleek, white yachts tugging at their moorings on the rising tide. It was a peaceful scenario, which veiled Mark's painful unease about what he would soon reveal. They had been talking about Susan's latest project, but she seemed to notice that something was on his mind.

They were on their second martini when out of nowhere he blurted, "Susan, what do you think about a divorce?"

She lowered her martini glass and eyed him over the rim. Her tanned skin blanched as the expression of shock overtook her. Her voice sounded small, almost hoarse. "My God, Mark. Did something happen on your trip? Why would you ask such a thing?" He knew her well enough to know her surprise and shock were genuine.

He almost immediately wished he had never said it. But it was too late now. He searched in vain for the right words. "No, no. It's been building for a long time."

Susan's eyes carefully scrutinized him. She was regarding him as though he were a stranger. "I know the sex isn't often, but after all we are getting older...."

That sounded so reasonable; he didn't know how to respond. Finally he said, "Well, yes, that's part of it. But there's more. I've been so...."

Her eyes were imploring him. "What?"

"I don't know," he said, gesturing vaguely with his hand as he tried to find the right words to say what was in his heart. "So unfulfilled."

Susan was silent for a moment. Their table was an oasis of tension in the quiet little restaurant. Finally, her voice resolute, she said, "Be honest with me, Mark. Is there another woman?"

He automatically stuttered, "No. Of course not. What are the chances that on a three-day trip to the East Coast I would find a woman, fall in love, and ask you for a divorce?"

The irony of his own words was ringing in his ears. But of course he had truly already been in love with Melanie for years.

Another silence ensued, this one more awkward. The tinkling of dinnerware and soft murmuring of other diners filled in the space. Then Susan, smiling, said, "Come on, Mark. You're probably just having a midlife crisis." She reached across the table and put her hand on top of his, squeezing it gently. "You know that time in life when older men start looking at pretty young girls in bikinis. They develop a need to run around in fancy sports cars, go to the gym every day, and dye their hair."

He contemplated her remarks carefully. *If only she knew what was really going on. Should I just tell her the whole truth?* But that would hurt her so badly, and he couldn't do that. Instead, he softly said, "Susan, we're a little beyond midlife, and I hope you know that I'm not so shallow a man that I would start ogling children."

"I didn't say children," she snapped. Then in a softer tone she added, "Young women today are way more mature than in my day, and they start looking at wealthy older men with an eye toward the future."

"No, I can assure you it's not that," Mark said emphatically, shaking his head slowly. "Besides, I consider myself way too old for such frivolous thinking."

"Too old?" Susan laughed, but without mirth. "No such thing. Not nowadays. Haven't you heard that sixty is the new fifty?"

He shook his head. "That's just some New Age blather. Tell that to my arthritis. Tell that to my worsening eyesight."

She offered a tepid smile. "Come on, sweetheart. We can't throw away so many years of successful marriage. We have to at least try. Don't you think? Divorce at our age is almost unthinkable. Unless," she said, "there really is another woman involved."

He cocked his head at that, knowing, innately that she had a point. "Well, I just don't know. What do you suggest?"

"My first thought is marriage counseling," Susan said sincerely.

He thought about that, and he didn't like the idea at all. What could some counselor say that they didn't both already know? He should have just rejected the idea out of hand. But he didn't. "Well that sounds reasonable," he replied quietly. "I almost thought you would be talking about one of those seminars up in the hills where you do Buddhist religious chants all morning, fast all day, and then go into a group and talk about your feelings."

She smiled. "So that's how you think of me. California hip and New Age."

He sipped on his drink. Not only did he abhor what he had just described, but the very idea of sitting and telling some strangers the most intimate details of his life was not appealing. Even divulging his thoughts one on one with a marriage counselor sounded unbearable.

Susan looked at him knowingly. "You don't like the counseling idea. I can understand that. But let's face it, the alternative is pretty grim. Think of our children. They'd be torn up. They're thinking about us doting on our grandchildren—not this."

She had to bring that up! he thought. She did know him well after all of these years. The kids were his one weakness. The very idea of hurting them in the slightest way was enough to push him into just about anything—even to marriage counseling, which Mark was all but certain was doomed to failure. Nonetheless, he thought, *my finding happiness doesn't seem to be as important as the unhappiness I would cause others if I left her.*

When they got home, both were quiet as they contemplated their new status in life: people on the verge of divorce. Their marriage problems loomed as an unpleasant reality, one that they now had to face head on.

This tension was all so new to him. He'd never before in his life had to worry about somebody else's feelings concerning his own marital relations, and he knew Melanie wouldn't take this well. When they'd parted, both had the subliminal (though unspoken) feeling that they would have a future together. And without really thinking about it, having such a future meant divorce for both of them. Sure, people got divorced all the time—but people their age?

The next afternoon, he called Melanie from his office. Both were energized at hearing each other's voices. Amidst all the excitement, his bad news that he had agreed to his wife's insistence about counseling came like a splash of cold water.

He now said, "What do you think?"

Silence. She hesitated, suddenly embarrassed, apparently, by her own neediness and vulnerability. "Well, I … I don't know. Surely you and your wife know what is best for you. I guess I was kind of carried away with it all. I don't even really know the status of my own marriage, or what my husband would say to the suggestion of divorce."

Her innocent remark gave him pause. He thought, *Here I am talking divorce with my wife, but Melanie isn't? What's with that?*

Still, he knew he had to handle things with sensitivity and finesse. After all, Melanie would be the last wife in his life.

"Yes," he said, trying not to betray too much emotion. "It's going to be more complicated than I thought. This is all pretty new and difficult to handle." But hearing the sadness and disappointment in her voice, he quickly added, "Look Melanie. In all honesty, I feel that counseling is just a formality prior to divorce. I'm already inclined in favor of a divorce. I would hope that you would be thinking the same thing."

While those comments were a salve to her aching heart, she also felt the need to defend her emotions and not seem so needy. She was so drawn to him; there was no doubt about that. In some ways, their pairing up seemed like perfection. Of course the perfection of this scenario was more of an emotional belief than an intellectual belief. Also, she noted some disappointment in his voice when she said she had done nothing about talking to her husband about divorce.

His voice brightened. "Look, I'm going to New York at the end of the month. Any chance we can meet there?"

Not wanting to seem overeager, she paused for a while. The phone line buzzed. But Melanie simply wasn't very good at disguising her ambivalence. "I uh … I think I might be able to make it. Of course I'd have to check with work.… Actually, I don't know right now."

When the telephone conversation ended, while there remained some hope for Melanie, she had a bittersweet feeling about it, too. The emotions were intense. He had crept into her psyche, and she was swallowing every bit of him, bringing him closer to her than she could ever imagine being to another human being.

By this time in Florida, the afternoon shadows had grown long. Melanie had sought out a favorite stretch of the beach near home. She walked, her feet splashing in the surf. It had been a bright, sunny day, and as evening approached, there were still only a few puffy clouds flying high. Gulls swooped and squealed as they circled above and then dived toward the water for their dinner. None of her thinking so far was guided by practical matters, although she tried to steer it that way. All she knew for sure was that she wanted him, and that she was too old to play games. Why kid herself? If she didn't go, she'd be forever wondering if she had passed up a life of hope, passion, and romance. She headed for home, determined to dash off an e-mail before she convinced herself to change her mind.

She wrote:

Honey,

I'll be there. Just tell me where and when. It can't be soon enough.

Melanie

Mark's reply came almost immediately:

You've made my day, babe! I will fill you in on the details as soon as my itinerary takes shape. Let me just tell you what's in my heart right now. I am feeling as if I am falling in love with you. And I can't wait to see you.

Mark

10

Melanie rode to the hospital for work with her convertible's top down. She was exhilarated by the wind on her face. But due to the unpredictable, late-summer Florida weather, she took the precaution of putting the top up before she went in the hospital.

The first indication that it was going to be a busy day was when a student nurse dashed up to her on the ward. "Come quickly, Melanie! Mr. Bradshaw in Room 12 must have had a reaction to his meds."

Melanie said, "Stay calm, Sue. I'll be right there. Meanwhile, get Doctor Collins."

As soon as Melanie dealt with this emergency, she headed for the break room for a cup of coffee and a quick message to Mark. It wasn't that she had anything in particular to say; she simply couldn't resist the urge to keep in touch with him and let him know that he was always in her thoughts. After all, he was the one who'd suggested she trade in her old phone for an updated version, making it easier for them to stay in touch with all the gadgets that the newer cell phones contained.

Good morning. Just thinking of you.
  Melanie

At the day's end, Melanie prepared to go home feeling good about the work she had put in. In addition to the

Bradshaw emergency, she had dealt with another near-fatal heart attack that had a good outcome. This work helped define her life and her place in society. She knew that she was successful at what she did, and this sense of accomplishment was a great contentment in her life.

On the way home, the idea came to her that she should buy some new clothes. Shopping wasn't her thing. She didn't like it because she couldn't tell what looked good on her and what didn't. When she shopped alone, torn with indecision, she usually wound up returning most of the items. Melanie needed Lois's practiced eyes. She dialed up her friend, who readily agreed to meet her at the mall.

Melanie did some window-shopping at the Victoria's Secret branch at the mall while waiting for Lois. In a daring mood, she bought a black lacy thong, having remembered that Mark had mentioned one. She also remembered that his motive hadn't been selfish, but he'd suggested that such a piece of lingerie would make her feel sexy. She tried it on in the dressing room, and she had to agree that Mark was right! Melanie felt a certain "naughtiness" that made her tingle. Of course it also made her feel a bit self-conscious, as if she were only half-dressed and without the support she was used to. She pictured the look in Mark's eyes when he'd see her dressed this way.

Caught up in the mood, she also bought a black, push-up bra, and she rejoiced in the carefree feeling of youth that allowed her to indulge herself. Liking what she saw in the mirror helped, too.

Lois arrived soon after and was impressed right away by Melanie's new uninhibited mood and was encouraged to help her to pick out even more daring new clothes. They found some cute casual clothes, short dresses, tight leggings, and sexy, low-cut tops.

For Lois, the shopping spree was a departure from her usual bargain-hunting at the discount stores. But with no trouble at all, Lois managed to get into this experience with her friend. It wasn't her money, anyway! Lois grinned, looking on as her friend tried each of the new outfits. "Lenny is going to love this," she said, quickly adding, "That is, if you care what he likes."

Melanie merely rolled her eyes and reached for the next garment. She was used to wearing nurse outfits during the day and casual comfortable clothes in the evening. These new clothes had nothing to do with her husband. She was doing this for herself. She felt herself blushing, knowing that also she was dressing up for Mark.

It was a blessing in her life that these days Lois, her old high school chum, lived nearby. For much of their lives, they had not been neighbors.

As they were taking a coffee break, having a latte at one of the many spots dotting the halls of the mall, Lois asked, "Do you think you will want to go to the fiftieth high school reunion next year?"

Some of the more enthusiastic schoolmates, too anxious to wait for the "big one," were having their own mini-reunions. Lois had been invited to several but had declined each one, for fear she wasn't cute enough and young enough to compete.

When Melanie declined to answer Lois's query right away, Lois grinned and said, "What, you're not anxious to compete with all that plastic surgery?"

Melanie grinned back. "Everybody in our class was beautiful. Remember Katie Green and Sarah Jennings? You have to admit, they'll be a hard act to follow."

Lois broke out into a full smile now. "Shoot. You'll give them all a run for their 'plastic-surgery money.'"

Melanie lapsed thoughtful. "I might do something, but I cringe at the idea of work on my eyes. No way on that." Brightening, she said, "Anyway I think I've found my own personal 'Fountain of Youth.'" She wondered—could it be that her very thoughts were youthful enough to give her a different look? Could her inner feelings change her outward packaging?

Lois smiled. "Never hurts to keep up with the competition."

"How about you?" Melanie asked. "Do you think you'll be going to the reunion?"

Lois shook her head. "Not my thing. I'm plenty busy with my husband, golf, my painting, and shopping. I've got plenty to keep me happy at home, and I have no curiosity about how the old gang is doing. As good as I am, I hope."

Because Melanie longed for the Northern climes, the two women often had discussions about Florida. Melanie lamented, "I miss New England and the four seasons. You know, the freshness of spring with everything blossoming. The brisk, pretty fall with all the leaves turning into vivid, russet colors. Weather that makes you feel alive, and then the winter with all the fun one can have in snow. I think I've used my fireplace twice since I've been in Florida," she sighed. "I do miss the change of season."

"Yeah, I know what you mean," Lois said. "But I don't live on memories, so I don't think of the things I miss. Rather, I think about the life I'm enjoying now. And as for those dreadful, stormy winters? No thank you! I'm so happy we are here." With a wistful look, Lois added, "I sure hope your longing for New England doesn't take you away from me."

Melanie thought about that for a moment and smiled, patting Lois's hand. "Don't worry, friend, I'm going to be around a while. Especially now that I have you." The two parted, considering the day's hunt to have been a success.

Once home, Melanie put her new "treasures" carefully away, then hurried through preparations for dinner. While the salmon was grilling, she checked her e-mail. Her heart pounded while she read it.

Babe,

Thinking of you. I'm making final scheduling for a trip to NYC. Big account coming up there.

Love for you to join me.

Interested?

Mark

This communication stopped her in her mental tracks. *Now what? Of course I want to go. I could say anything to Lenny—going home to visit relatives; whatever.* At the moment, she couldn't concern herself too much with the logistics. It was all about following her heart. She had read somewhere that the heart was a lonely hunter. *It's true,* she thought. *As exciting as all of this is, it is all bottled up. Each decision is one I have to make alone. And* it is *a lonely thing.* She immediately typed out a reply. Her answer was a resounding and enthusiastic yes.

Dinner with Lenny was the usual uneventful and perfunctory ten-minute affair. She tried to make conversation, but most of the time her efforts seemed to fall on deaf ears. Soon she found herself alone, doing the dishes, while he was off on some pursuit of his own. She remembered one of her first dates with Lenny, when they just couldn't get enough of each other and sneaked away from the party to be alone. *I guess we were just smitten with each other,* she thought. *But did we really know each other? It felt right and we jumped.*

Suddenly her thoughts turned to her kids. Guilt swept over her for not spending enough time with them. After all, no matter how old they were, they would always be her children. Moreover, they were not only a connection to her past, but also a connection to her very being, a lifeline to her soul. She missed them both. Her soul longed for their company.

She phoned her daughter, Meaghan, in Brookline. Meaghan answered immediately. Upon hearing Melanie's voice, Meaghan's enthusiasm picked up. "Hi Mom. It's great to hear from you."

Melanie pictured her beautiful daughter, and she smiled. "Thanks, hon; you, too. So how are things in Brookline? I heard the good old Commonwealth of Massachusetts is getting set for another hard winter. And my cute little granddaughter; I miss her so."

"Oh, I haven't heard any predictions for the winter. But a hard one would be nothing new. We're used to the mean old Yankee winter. As for Allison, she gets cuter each day and is smart as a whistle. You're gonna love this, Mom, and I'm glad you called. I was about to call you, but I know you are so busy at work I thought I'd wait until the weekend." Melanie prepared for some important news. The young woman continued, "You know how Jim and I have been talking about how nice it would be to get out of this cold, nasty Northeast?"

"Yes, but—"

"But nothing. Jim has a transfer to NASA, and we're coming to Florida to live. Specifically, Delray Beach. Basically right up the road from you."

Melanie's face lit up. "Oh, honey, that's great. We can—"

Meaghan interrupted, "That's right, Mom, we can raise this new baby together! I'm now almost a mother of two, and I could really use your support."

Melanie reached for a hankie to dab at her eye. She was so emotional that she had to stifle a sob. "Meaghan, that's such great news! I couldn't be happier. Have you told your brother yet?"

"As a matter of fact I did. I had a long talk with Eddie just last night."

"How are things with him?"

'Oh, the computer nerd of Silicon Valley is doing great. Making piles of money and changing the world."

Melanie's voice lapsed nostalgic—or was it melancholy? "Great. I miss you guys so much sometimes."

Her daughter's voice took on a different tone. "How's it going with you, Mom? Lenny still the same old selfish oaf?"

"Don't say that, Meaghan." Melanie almost choked on lack of sincerity. "I guess he tries."

"Yeah, right. Meaning he tries to get out to the golf course as fast as he can. Eddie feels the same as I do. You're way too good for him. Dad might not have been great, but this guy is the pits. I wish you'd leave him, and find someone who deserves you and would treat you like the princess that you are."

There was an awkward silence on the phone. Finally Meaghan said, "Good, you're thinking about it."

"Now wait a minute, Meaghan, I—"

"Yeah, I know. I can tell. You're thinking about it."

Just then Melanie heard Lenny's car leaving the driveway. She said, "Wait a sec." When she got back with Meaghan, she said, "It was Lenny leaving."

"Where's he going?" Meaghan asked.

"I don't know. I don't really keep track of his comings and goings. Oh, yes—it's his Monday night poker game with the boys."

"See what I mean. Another one of his hobbies. Does he spend any time with you?"

"Don't worry about it, Darling. I don't need male companionship like I did at your age. I don't care what he does."

Meaghan's irritation came through the phone line. Melanie could almost see that nervous habit Meaghan had of twirling a strand of blonde hair when she was upset.

"You're just saying that," Meaghan countered, "because you have no choice in the matter. If you asked him to spend more time at home, you know he wouldn't do it."

"That's not true, Meg. It's like I said, I really don't care."

"Wasn't that one of the main reasons you divorced Dad? He lost interest in your relationship?"

"Yes, along with other things—the affair he had didn't help. Even though I was willing to forgive him. People make mistakes. If they're willing to be responsible, remorseful, and walk a straighter line, I think everyone deserves a second chance."

"I do miss Dad," Meaghan said.

"Yes, he was good father to you kids. It is a shame that he didn't get more time."

"The older I get," Meaghan said, "the more I realize that when he died of a brain tumor at fifty, he wasn't very old. He had never been ill in his life and survived a tour in Vietnam with nothing more than a cut from some elephant grass."

"Perhaps the years of heavy drinking did not allow him to be strong enough to put up much of a fight," Melanie said.

"Both Eddie and I realize that Dad was an alcoholic and cheated on you. But that was Dad's behavior, not Lenny's. How do you know Lenny doesn't feel bad about the way he has been neglecting you? Does he get a second chance?"

"I don't know how Lenny feels. We don't talk about our feelings. But he doesn't have the history that your Dad and I had."

"Hmmph. Sounds to me like you don't care one way or another."

Melanie let a little silence hang on the phone line. Then she said, "You might be right, Meg. But enough of this kind of unpleasant talk. When are you guys coming? Give me all the details. Are you going to rent or buy a place? I was thinking that if Eddie came here, we could have ourselves a lovely little reunion."

"We don't have it all figured out yet. But the good part is that I can be very close to you. The NASA facility is right near you. And I'll have little Junior down there."

"Junior? You know?"

"Oh yeah. My husband insisted."

"You kids. A boy—a little brother for Allison. How wonderful! In my day, we had to wait for the big day to find out."

They talked for another forty minutes. When Melanie hung up, ambivalent emotions tumbled over her. What if she and Mark got married and she had to move to California? A fantasy, for sure—but if it panned out, all those beautiful plans she had just made with her daughter would be out the window. *Why do things have to be so complicated?* But she slowed herself down. Who knew if her relationship with Mark was going to lead to marriage? Further, is marriage what she really wanted? And moreover, did she even know what she wanted? In any case, Lenny was the last of her considerations. He had earned her lackadaisical attitude toward him by the offhanded way he had been treating her and their marriage these past years.

Melanie made herself a drink. Her thoughts drifted back to the night she and Mark had spent together. She had to admit, as wrong as the world said that adultery was, the thought of that night's lovemaking sent a thrill up her spine. The drink made her sleepy, so she went to bed and dreamed of Mark.

11

The day dawned bright. When she awoke, she felt light-hearted and exuberant. She looked at herself in the mirror. She knew this face. *But there are fewer lines under my eyes? How could that be?* She was under more tension than usual. But she felt different. *Younger? Yes, that was it.* She had a different look. *What was it?* She had heard it in a song somewhere: "Your eyes are the eyes of a woman in love." Above all, Melanie had longed to be a woman in love, one who couldn't wait to be in the arms of her lover.

The excitement was thrilling and addictive. She told Lenny that she was going to visit her daughter, and as usual, he could barely care less.

On the way to the airport, her thoughts churned in confusion. *Yes,* she thought, *there is strong chemistry and a physical attraction between me and Mark. But we need something more. Something that will sustain us over the long haul. But isn't that the reason for this trip—to see if we connect on a deeper level? Is he really the soul mate I have always wanted? Or is it all just an ego trip? Or maybe both!* Doubts crept into the logical corners of her psyche. *Why am I going? Is it because Lois said it was in my stars?* She cocked her head and took a deep breath. *That's not an intelligent reason. Even a goofy schoolgirl wouldn't think that was a good enough reason to pursue Mark.*

Maybe I'm kidding myself. Probably I would be better off just going on with my life. This existence with Lenny isn't great, but it isn't so bad, either. However, if I don't go, all I lose is a plane ticket. And, infinitely more importantly, my newfound youth.

She needed to call Mark. She wanted to involve him in her angst. Maybe he could shed some light on her confused thoughts. There was still plenty of time before takeoff. Being early was always one of Melanie's positive traits.

When she parked the car, she headed for a quiet spot to phone Mark. She ended up having to text him to call her back; that was their arrangement. Waiting impatiently, she collected her thoughts—what to say and how to say it. The phone rang. It was him.

She blurted, "Mark, I'm sorry to bother you but I am having trouble with my thoughts."

"Mel, are you having those two-way conversations again?"

"Sort of. I don't think I should come to New York. All of this has happened so fast for us. Maybe we were both so needy that we weren't in our right minds. Now I am being so deceptive to my husband, and I'm wondering for what—and if this relationship is going anywhere."

When he answered her, she was thrilled by the resolute tone in his voice. She clung to every word. "I am crazy about you," he started out. "That is all I know right now. But I understand your feelings. I came so suddenly into your life and created a whole new world for you. I'm sorry, babe. I'll be devastated if you don't come, but I will still be longing for you. You decide. Maybe we need to have this time in New York to check it out, to see what there really is between us. If it happens for real, then we will discuss options. Anyway, isn't this a chance for you to go back home for a bit? It allows us to visit our old stomping grounds, too. It was a combined trip, so you don't have to feel guilty about it. Aren't you planning to see your daughter?"

She let that idea sink in, then murmured, "Mark, you excite me to all limits. Hearing your voice sends me to another planet. That is my problem: I *want* to get on the plane."

She recognized excitement in his voice. "Then do it. I want you to come. Can't wait to see you. Text me when you land."

"Mark, are you sure? I know I might drive you crazy with my anxious feelings, but this quandary is for real. Promise me: We'll talk it through?"

"No doubt," he assented. "Anything you want."

When she hung up, she knew she would be going, though she was still plagued with a lot of questions and fears.

Flying wasn't her fondest mode of transportation. She was a white-knuckle flyer and had feared it most of her life. But there was no other way to go. At the moment, her passion trumped her fear, and she was ready. She still tingled from the memory of his voice, and she was willing to do anything to be with him, even sit terrified at over 30,000 feet. As she sat in the coach section of the aircraft, she was in limbo, with thoughts of Mark. By the time they were airborne and the earth was dropping away, she still wasn't aware of the sensation of flight.

She hadn't told Meaghan that she would be visiting, although she probably should have. But Melanie was optimistic that it would be a good surprise. She missed her daughter and grandchild very much. She couldn't wait to get the cute little girl in her arms. Her son was so wrapped up in his fast California lifestyle that she didn't expect any grandchildren from him for a while. So Meaghan was her only hope for little ones. And now there was going to be another one to hold and to spoil. Melanie knew Meaghan was going to be thrilled to see her.

Deep in her thoughts about all the changes in her life, she hardly noticed the plane's descent into the New York area. The flight attendant suddenly announced, "Welcome to New York. The weather is clear, and the temperature in the high seventies. Enjoy your stay."

She retrieved her luggage: a medium-sized, light-green case. She headed for the cab stand for the short ride into the city. She texted Mark as he had requested. As her cab navigated the canyons of Manhattan, she returned to her thoughts. *Wow, a new baby. How weird was this? At the same time, me, at my age, once again turning into a sexual being.*

His call brought her back. "Hi babe. I'm so glad you came. I am excited to see you. Do you have the directions? Get comfortable when you get to the hotel, and I will be there shortly. I am finishing up with a new client."

She wanted to talk, yet she didn't want to drain the tremendous anticipation that she sensed he was feeling—not to mention her own expectancy. "See you soon," was all that she could manage to say.

The hotel was beyond first class. This extravagance made her feel special; she knew he'd spared no cost. Not even using the elevator could dampen her mood. Once at the room, she changed into something sexy. She marveled at her new image, her new feelings, and her lack of inhibition. *Does he really think I'm pretty?* Melanie was so concerned about her appearance that wanting to be perfect for him became an obsession. After all, Susan was so beautiful, that Melanie often wondered why he was choosing her instead. This still didn't make much sense to her. Mark's life was almost a fairy tale, and yet he wanted her?

In no time, he was at the door. She stood in the doorway as he drank her in, his eyes exploring every inch of her. His hungry gaze made her come near to a blush. Their kiss was otherworldly. She was sure she had never been kissed that way before: tongues swimming back and forth, the lust deepening. Clearly, it would be foolish to give this up. She threw herself into the new reality and at least for the moment, ceased thinking practically.

"You look great, Mel," he gushed. "Do you like the room? I hope I didn't disappoint you with my choice."

"Mark, it's perfect. But then again, so are you."

He smiled. "Stop it. If you keep stroking my ego like that, I won't be able to handle it. I see myself as a very ordinary guy."

"It's just that in my eyes, you are so special. Why do you think I'm here?"

"I hope you're hungry," he said. "I picked out a quiet place in Little Italy. Hope it's okay. You did say you wanted to talk, right?"

"How did you know I love Little Italy?"

"I guess I sense something Italianate about you. Maybe it's one of those outstanding and beautiful Modiglianis I've seen at the museum. Besides, your passion is infectious."

He ordered a fine wine from room service and poured them each a glass. They sipped it while they viewed the spectacular Manhattan skyline. They could see beyond the tall skyscrapers, all the way to the great bend in the Hudson. It was dusk, and the lights were starting to pop on all over town.

They sipped the rest of their wine as they rode the elevator down to the lobby. Mark ordered a cab from the concierge. The man smiled at the happy couple and Mark tipped him well.

The restaurant wasn't crowded yet, because Manhattanites dine late. There were still a lot of tables left, with their red-and-white checkered tablecloths. The couple sat down and perused the menu. He ordered for her, and his choices seemed to suggest that he was choosing a meal that would be setting a romantic mood. Her eyes popped when the dish arrived. She cocked her head at him.

He smiled and said, "It's *pollo agradolce,* a unique yet subtle sweet and sour chicken dish."

She beamed, curious. "And you picked it because…?"

"I picked it because it is unique. It's a delicate dish with overtones that are uncertain, yet irresistible." She gazed at him, and he added quietly, "Like you."

Throughout the wonderful meal, Melanie ran her shoeless foot up under Mark's pant leg and up his shin. She knew how much he liked it, and this kind of flirtation sent a thrill up her own leg as well. It was totally out of character for her, which was precisely why it felt so good now. She totally forgot her anxieties, and she did not mention them.

After dinner they wandered the streets of the Village, hand in hand, the lively conversation never going where Melanie had planned. When she was with him, all her plans didn't seem important enough to break the spell.

When they grabbed a cab back to the hotel, her heart began to race. She couldn't keep her hands off him.

Once in the room, he swept her into his arms and kissed her. It was a kiss filled with longing (more than passion), and she was drunk with it. When he released her, they fell on the bed. She didn't remember getting undressed, just the endless kisses, the soft murmuring, and the exploration of her body with his voracious lips.

Every time she thought she was ready to burst, he slowed down and continued to caress her, murmuring his adoration of her body. She lost track of time, and she couldn't get enough. Their bodies had melded into one; there was no telling where one began and the other ended. He was gentle, yet demanding, making her feel like she wanted to submit to any and all of his desires. He knew where and how to touch her, and he had discovered where she would feel the most tingle. He started at the top and worked his way down, deftly using his mouth and hands, not leaving anything to her imagination. He stirred her up, making her wet and wild. The feeling of him deep inside her was warm and penetrating. He was leaving his essence in her, and she wanted it badly. She wanted to take it home with her. She hoped for days on end to walk around remembering the feeling of him deeply inside her. When they finally released each other, they were covered in a patina of mist, both gasping for breath, both lost in another dimension. She never wanted to be anywhere else, or be anyone else. Like magic, he made her feel all-woman and young at heart.

They slept intertwined most of the night. He had pulled her into his embrace, wrapping his arms around her so that she was facing away from him in a spooning position, drifting off into a magical place.

In the morning, she awoke to bright sunshine flooding the room. She found him gazing at her with adoring eyes. She subconsciously pulled the sheet up closer, covering her breasts. He said, "I have something for you. After last night, I'm sure that we both know why I want you to have it. It's something that when you wear it, you'll know I'm wearing its mate."

He showed her two very simple bracelets made of stainless steel with a rubber link. The two bracelets were the same, only his had a more masculine heft to it. He told her that when he purchased them, he had no idea why he was buying two. Was it planned in the stars that he would want to share the second bracelet with her one day? After all, he could only wear one!

Tears filled her eyes as he clasped her bracelet around her wrist. She held it up to the sunlight, admiring its shine, while he continued to gaze at her, his eyes smiling with love.

And then, too soon, they had to say good-bye. Melanie was thrust back into the reality of her life.

She headed for the train that would take her to visit her daughter. The steady click-clack of the train rolling north to Boston lulled her into a daze. The time with Mark had been so great that they never did get around to any serious talk about their relationship. They were too busy being star-struck lovers, gazing into each other's eyes and cozying up to each other through the night. She had this warm feeling of him inside her, and she felt full and complete. The train ride gave her the time to remember his caresses, long for him, and guess about the next step. Just as she wondered how he was feeling, she saw another e-mail:

You excite me to the extremes of consciousness. I dream of our next date. You are wet and I am big. Life has no limits.

And that told her all that she needed to know.

By the time she reached Boston and took a cab to Brookline, she had come to one undeniable conclusion: Whatever else might happen to them in the future, today she and Mark were a couple. A duo. A pair. Still, the important questions had not been answered.

Meaghan's mouth turned into a large O when she opened the door and saw her mother. She shrieked, "You're here. You didn't tell me," and she flew into her mother's arms. Ali was right behind her, and she, too, was immediately in Grandma's arms.

While her daughter brewed coffee, Melanie's thoughts grew melancholy. She remembered how it felt to be a young woman in the prime of life. At the time, Melanie had overwhelming feelings of love and devotion to her husband and her marriage. Of course the bad part came eventually— the pain of betrayal, followed by divorce, and finally his death at fifty from cancer, which their son Eddie had taken particularly hard. But by the time the coffee was ready, Melanie's sad thoughts dissipated. Her memories drifted back to that sweeter part of life, and for the moment, she was lost in the wonder of first love.

The two women had much to talk about, considering a new baby was coming and Meaghan's family was moving to Florida. Melanie and her daughter related so well to each other that at times the line between parent and child blurred. Even physically, they might be mistaken for a younger sister and an older sister. Sometimes it was difficult for Melanie to maintain the image of parental authority and wisdom.

Melanie realized that her relationship with Mark would soon force her to put all of her cards on the table. At her age, this might be the last time she would be in love.

12

Melanie couldn't keep her gaze from Meaghan: her beauty, her grace, and her bubbly personality. Always in awe of her lovely daughter, Melanie could not help being amazed at Meaghan's cheerfulness and charm.

In the meantime, Meaghan was marveling at her mother's looks and youthful energy. "Mom, I don't know how you do it. If I didn't know better, I'd say you'd had some work done. There's not a lady your age in town who hasn't had something done."

Melanie responded wistfully, "Don't think I haven't considered it, but the very thought of a scalpel near my face gives me the willies. I would love to get my eyes done, but all my consultations of plastic surgeons have scared me to death. No, I'm not going that route."

"Well shoot, Mom. You don't have to. Why consider it? Geez, if I could look like you at your age, I don't think I could be more satisfied."

"Thank you, darling. But I'm sure all the popular girls from my grade will look much better than I would at the reunion—which is why I probably won't go. You're being too kind, Meg."

"No, I'm not."

This kind of talk made Melanie wonder if she should discuss her life dilemma with her daughter. On the one hand, she would appreciate any feedback; but on the other hand, it would negate her role as a parent. Asking a child, even as an adult, for personal advice, seemed out of place. She had always been very close to Meaghan, and at times the boundaries had been blurred; but this was too big. She really wanted to just blurt it out, but she worried that it was too much with which to burden a daughter.

Meaghan did bring up Lenny. "How's it going with Lenny, Mom?" As she waited for an answer, she added, "Or should I ask?"

"Thanks for asking, darling. Well, it's much the same."

"Meaning you sit home alone, while he plays golf and cards with his friends."

"Pretty much."

The young woman frowned. "How can you stand that? If I didn't have someone to talk to at night about my feelings after my long days of just being a mom, I think I'd flip. It's good that I get to work a bit and be with adults; but being with my husband is so special, I just crave time with him."

"Well, for me, it's just become a habit—a bad one, I must say! And at my stage in life, what is there? Although recently I have been dressing younger and feeling younger. Don't know why, though. But it is helping."

Meaghan reached over and took her hand. "I think I understand, Mom. It's more like a matter of commitment."

Melanie smiled at her child's intuitive character. "Yeah, that's it. I don't feel that we're a ..." She had to search her heart for clarity. "I guess I don't feel that we're a couple. We're just two people who live together."

Meaghan quickly changed the subject. She was full of ideas for the day. Melanie would have been content simply to play with her adorable granddaughter, Ali, but Meaghan had other plans.

"Hey, let's do some shopping. I'm having a baby. He is going to need all kinds of stuff. Ali loves the pizza place at the Chestnut Hill Mall. How does that sound?" She rambled on so fast that before Melanie could answer, Meaghan was already bundling up the toddler and her traveling baggage.

Melanie paid a lot of attention to Ali during the drive. The child was the mirror image of her mother: cornflower blue eyes, wet straw blonde hair—the kind that on an adult like Meaghan looked so natural, no hint of having gotten that color out of a bottle. Meaghan smiled and enjoyed watching her mother interact with the child. Melanie was so in tune with Ali and so young at heart herself. She often wished she could have the child all to herself for a while. She always relived the days when Meaghan was small, and she was just a mom. Too bad she had stopped at two children; but then again, they were both awesome.

As they drove through various neighborhoods, Melanie watched her surroundings, lost in days gone by. She had some déjà vu reminiscences as she took in the sights and sounds of her old stomping grounds, predominantly Jewish Brookline. She saw the old-style delis, reminiscent of their New York beginnings, the beautiful townhouses along maple-lined streets, the orange cars of the "T" rumbling down the middle of Chestnut Hill Avenue, the eclectic cluster of buildings at Boston College, ranging from a towering Gothic cathedral to fifties-style architecture.

By the time they got to the Chestnut Hill Mall, which was an ultra-modern center, Melanie had already taken a trip back to many girlhood memories.

At the mall, they had a wonderful time picking out baby outfits and baby gear. Melanie insisted on paying for all of it. Ali had been so good through it all, but she kept asking when she could ride the merry-go-round. Both women were tired but couldn't refuse her, so they made their way to the merry-go-round. The magical sounds of the ride, along with the beautiful designs of the horses, were never taken for granted. It was a moment of childhood for all of them. After the third time around, all three of them were tired and hungry.

"Where'd you like to go for lunch, Mom?"

"I thought Ali wanted pizza?"

"Yes she did, so let's indulge her."

"I was looking at the delis on the way here, and my mouth began watering for some deli food. I can almost taste the knishes, the smoked salmon, the lox, and bagels. But I can get those back in Boca, of course. It may not be quite the same, but I can deal! Ali takes precedence now."

"Jim and I were planning on taking you out for dinner tonight. As the guest, it should be your choice. It was supposed to be a surprise. He was flabbergasted that you were here when I called him at work."

"He's such a sweetheart. Okay, deli tonight, but pizza right now at the food court for Ali."

Meaghan rolled her eyes. "Okay. On the upper level, they have a spectacular little cafe. Next time we will go there."

Meaghan revisited the topic of the reunion. "So do you really think you will forego the big one?" she asked.

"I think I'll skip it. Actually, all of the reunion talk has sparked some mini-reunions of eight to ten people. A mini reunion might be more to my liking, and I will have fewer of those surgical queens to deal with. I've talked to Lois about it, and although she's not interested in attending, she keeps trying to get me to go. I do not know why she wants me to go when she is not going."

"Is Lois still into astrology?"

"Is she! She always has advice for me. And she continually asks me to let her do my chart. I think she secretly has done it already, because she keeps coming up with new information about my future."

"Like how to make life with Lenny better?"

"No, not exactly. You know Lois, she's always exploring relationships—that is, new relationships for me. How to make another—" she stopped.

Meaghan's brows raised.

"Oh you know, silly romance stuff. Lois is like that." Struggling to change the subject, Melanie said, "As for the reunion, one day I'm for it, but the next day I'm against it. I don't know. I think the class is getting too involved in the whole thing. Most of them are retired and don't have anything else to do. Sometimes it just doesn't seem that important. On one hand, I would look forward to going shopping for a whole new wardrobe. You know, things that will make me look younger."

"Come on, Mom. You don't need that. Not at all."

"Nice to hear from you, darling. Thank you. But seriously, I am ambivalent about making the trip."

Meaghan just rolled her eyes and poo-pooed her.

After their light but delightful lunch, they returned to Meaghan's house so that Ali could take a nap. Melanie was feeling a little tired, between the traveling and the "festivities" with Mark the day before. She kidded, "I don't work this hard at work."

That evening Meaghan got a babysitter so that they could go out to dinner. In the car, Jim, eager to impress, suggested a fine Boston restaurant. Meaghan broke in, "Mom has her mouth set for a good old-fashioned Jewish deli."

"Oh sure," he agreed readily. "There's no lack of them in town."

Melanie loved the way Jim brightened to other people's suggestions. For her, that was a rare quality. Of course she had always admired Jim, a good-looking, hard-working guy who made her daughter happy.

They settled on a nearby place. When they walked in, Melanie soaked in the very aroma of the deli. There was no formal dining; rather, the place was a cafeteria-style bonanza of Jewish delicacies, from lox and bagels to huge, dark-bread pastrami sandwiches and fat, sour Kosher pickles.

Meaghan said, "Mom, you look like you're in heaven."

"I am."

"Don't they have delis in Florida?" Jim inquired.

"Yes, but not like here."

They all laughed and dug in to a veritable feast of deli favorites.

Melanie had a barrage of questions about the move, which she aimed at Jim. "Does NASA give fathers paternity leave?"

Meaghan lifted her eyes skyward. "Sensitive questions, Mom. Mr. Work Horse here is so into his work, that he doesn't even want to take time off."

Getting defensive, Jim said, "Come on, Meggie. I said I'd see what I could do. It's not off the board. I'll take what I can. We're right in the middle of the Mars Rover program. It's historic and cutting-edge stuff."

Meaghan smiled and hugged his arm. "It's okay, Big Guy. Leave me home alone with a screaming infant while you conquer new worlds."

Everybody laughed. Meaghan said, "Good thing I'm gonna have Mom nearby to help out."

Melanie nodded in agreement, saying, "So you'll be moved in well before the baby is born?"

The young couple nodded together.

"That's just wonderful. It'll be so nice to have my daughter around. I can't wait for you to get down there."

The next day, Melanie was already teary-eyed at having to leave them. The upside was that Meaghan and her family were coming to Florida. That thought made saying goodbye a bit easier.

While Melanie was sitting in the airline lounge at Logan Airport, her phone rang. She didn't hear it at first because her thoughts were miles away; she had been psyching herself up for the flight back to Florida.

It was Mark. She was in a relatively quiet section of the terminal, so she had no trouble hearing him. He started out by saying, "How was your visit with your daughter?" But there was something "off" in his tone of voice, she thought.

Before Melanie could launch into a review of the visit, he had some bad news for her. She could sense his anxiety, because in the short time they had been together since those high school days of merely passing each other by, she had come to sense his moods. "Look, Melanie, this is hard to talk about, but there's been a development here."

"You finally told your wife about us?" In the back corners of her mind, Melanie was at once uncertain whether or not that was what she hoped to hear.

"I didn't mention you per se. Here's the thing. She knows that I'm interested in a divorce. But remember, she wants counseling."

Melanie swallowed hard. "And you're considering it?"

"Not really, but there are other issues involved now. You see, my oldest son, who is in business in Chicago, called. He's having serious business and financial problems. There's a real danger that he might lose everything."

"That's terrible," Melanie said with genuine concern. "What's happened?"

"Well, it's too complicated to explain on the phone, but the bottom line is—"

"Yes?"

"I don't feel comfortable putting yet another burden on my family by continuing with the divorce."

"So..." she said, letting her thought trail off.

"So I'm suggesting that we cool it. At least until this problem with my son comes to some kind of conclusion. He might even come home for a while."

Melanie felt his dilemma because she was a kind, compassionate woman. She said, "This must be upsetting you, Mark, as I know how important your family is to you. I hope it isn't too bad for him. I know you will be there for him every step of the way. But, I can't help but thinking about us. Only two days ago, we were together without a care in the world, or so it seemed. I know we didn't have any set plans for a future, but I felt we were heading somewhere special. I guess family problems really do change things."

"I'm sure this is hard on you but I …" The phone suddenly went dead.

In a nano second, black thoughts raced through her mind. She wasn't thinking of technical phone line problems, but of the promise of her new romance becoming a memory of yesterday.

Did he hang up?

Then he came back on, but with static. It finally cleared up, and she heard him say, "I must be in a bad cell area."

By now she was so discouraged that she just begged off and said, "I'm at the airport. I can't talk much now. I'll email you when I get home to Boca."

She heard him say, "Babe, don't go and have those conversations in your head again. I really want you. Although you can't be the main course at present, we will just have to settle for dessert."

Dessert? What was he talking about? She was rather abrupt hanging up, which fit her mood. She was hurt and confused. *Maybe it was better when my boring old life wasn't so complicated.*

13

She had her usual pre-flight jitters. Not until the aircraft was airborne did she think about Mark. He had told her that he needed to concentrate on family problems. It was a noble trait, living his life for others; he was a sweet, caring man. His strength of character was enviable. In contrast, she wondered about her own ethics. She wondered, *Am I simply succumbing to my overactive imagination and the needs of the flesh?* He was being the good and responsible parent. *How could she fault him for that?* Yet the abrupt halt to the relationship gnawed at her. She upbraided herself for being shallow and selfish. She vacillated between tears, anger, and understanding; but at this point, the understanding was running dead last to the tears and anger.

By the time she was flying over Washington, DC, she had decided that she should have stayed home. But wasn't it to her credit that she still had romantic longing, her heart throbbing with desire to be in his arms again? Her self-esteem was so much better lately because of his attention and nonjudgmental acceptance. No, it was impossible now to ignore the sexual arousal she felt every time she thought of him. She just didn't want to give up these exciting feelings, and she wouldn't. She would wait it out for now.

The flight landed. Melanie headed for home, and she was prepared for her life to revert right back to the same old grind. When she got home, Lenny was there. But what caught her by surprise was that he seemed excited to see her.

He was actually interested in the trip and wanted to talk about it. In order to get his mind off the trip, Melanie suggested going out to dinner.

At dinner, he again asked her about the trip. "How was New York? And Meaghan? I bet you were glad to be there seeing Ali again."

Caught off-guard, she focused on having seen Ali. "Yes, Ali is just the cutest thing. We went to the mall and took her on the merry-go-round. She really is quite smart, reading already, and she has such a good vocabulary for a four-year-old. I am just crazy about her. I can't wait until they move here. Did I forget to tell you about that?"

"No, you did mention it," Lenny reminded her. "So did you meet any of your high school classmates?"

"Yes, we met in Little Italy for dinner and shared some stories about teachers, football games, and who was going out with whom."

"So who was there? Anyone you told me about?"

This unsettled her even more. She really needed to do some fancy footwork to get out of this line of questioning. She said, "Oh some of the more fringe people, the ones I really wasn't that friendly with. It seems like the 'nerds' then, are the big shots now. They have become doctors, lawyers, and wealthy businessmen, even some into the world of Hollywood. You know, producers and directors. We had a lot of very smart kids. Impressive, but boring."

She hoped that this explanation would be the end of it, but he came back at her once again.

"So why did you meet them, then?"

"Well, I thought my best friend was going to be there." Taking the opportunity to encourage his interest, she added, "It's so nice of you to be interested, honey."

This little charade got her thinking: *So this new, inquisitive Lenny comes along when I have just about written our marriage off. Does this mean there is still hope for my marriage?*

She was perplexed. She hadn't thought Lenny was capable of being interested in her. What would life be like if Lenny suddenly was thoughtful and attentive to her? So by the time she got home, her plans were in limbo, to say the least. Still, she managed to e-mail Mark this much:

Mark,

I have been thinking about us for a while today. My return home was uneventful, except for the complication that my husband was unusually inquisitive about my trip. I had to dodge his questions, and lying didn't feel so good. I've been thinking about our last phone call, and about your reference to our relationship as dessert. Not too sure I totally get what you mean—but here is what I took away.

It is probably premature to think of our relationship as the main course. What we have now is special, which is certainly like a dessert. Remember, though, that although dessert is momentarily pleasurable, it doesn't have any lasting nutritional value. I guess that is all I can count on for now.

Are we better off without the drama we are causing in each other's lives? I don't want to cause you angst, but I have fallen in love with you, big time. I do not regret it. Even in the short time we have been together, I see my life changing, both within myself and outwardly. I thank you for that. You will have a lasting effect on me, for sure. So do what you need to do, and I will keep you in my thoughts.

Lovingly,
Melanie

She pushed the send button and got ready for bed. Tomorrow was a work day, but she would phone Lois and arrange a latte so she could fill her in.

Lois had a busy schedule, so Melanie had to be flexible. Because Lois heard the urgency in her friend's voice, she made it a priority to set up a coffee date. It was the season Melanie loved; pumpkin-spice lattes were back as a seasonal favorite—her favorite, too.

Lois listened intently as Melanie recounted the events of the past week. Lois was, of course, interested in Meaghan and Ali. When Meaghan was growing up, Meaghan had called her "Aunt Lois."

Melanie then began to talk about Mark. Melanie was surprised when Lois had plenty to say on that topic: "Mel, while you didn't know it, I have been following the transits to your natal chart. The challenging side of Uranus is transiting your seventh house. So, there can be unexpected surprises with close relationships. Further," Lois pointed out with a dramatic flourish, "Uranus is opposing your natal Neptune in your first house."

"Can you say that in English?" Melanie asked.

"Well, your first house describes yourself. Neptune in your first house denotes you as being an idealistic person. Being that you are a Libra, you are idealistic about relationships. Right now there can be unforeseen challenges to your relationships. These challenges can 'zap' your idealism and confuse you. What Mark said about dessert came as an unexpected surprise to you. His image zapped your idealism about the relationship."

Lois had her full attention now. Melanie said, "Tell me more about these 'houses.'"

"In every natal chart, there are twelve houses. Each house refers to the specific area of life that is affected by the particular planet in it. The planet is the energy, and the sign is how that planet's energy will be expressed."

Trying to absorb it, Melanie asked, "Anything else?"

"Yes, one more thing. You do have Jupiter in the ninth house. Jupiter is the planet of opportunity. This situation means that it is possible you will have an opportunity to travel."

"Wow, this stuff is really mind-boggling. I can see why you have studied it so hard," Melanie said to her friend. "I am not really into this astrology stuff, as you know, but I have heard that it is a very deep self-analysis. I guess it has a lot of merit."

A few days passed, and Melanie hadn't heard a word from Mark. Thinking a lot about what Lois had said made her feel somewhat uneasy. Having all those planets moving around made her feel like her life was being controlled.

She had settled back into her routine and was feeling lost, abandoned, and sad. She tried to keep her chin up and hoped Mark was working out his family problems. But what if these problems brought him closer to Susan? He might ultimately leave Melanie at the curb. Nonetheless, she really didn't want to suffocate him with e-mails, so she waited. Then this e-mail arrived:

Babe,

Sorry for the delay, but I have been busy. I've also been thinking of you and processing your e-mail. It seems like we do need to take a break and wait this out. I will keep you informed of the home situation, as I do my best to be there for everyone. Let's keep the e-mails going on, but only on an as-needed basis. I have to focus on the family now. If you need me to call, just let me know, and I will try.

Madly in love with you,
m.a.

He often ended e-mails with his initials, a trait uniquely his.

Melanie viewed this e-mail as an indication that her worst nightmare had come true. That he was pulling away was devastating, and her mood rapidly changed from excitement to despair. But she wasn't entirely surprised, as he had forewarned her with the message he'd sent while she was in the airport. Melanie had been too optimistic that Mark wouldn't be able to live without her, and she thought he would reconsider.

She resolved that it was time to take the trip to Paris of which she had been dreaming.. After all, Lois had said that Jupiter was in her ninth house, which meant travel!

She quickly dashed of an e-mail of her own:

> *Thank you, honey, for your honesty. I am devastated and will miss you terribly. It may be time for me to do some soul searching; and as you know, I am not only in love with you but with a city as well. I think I hear Paris calling.*
>
> *Take care, be happy, and do your family thing. I will be here for you.*
>
> *Mel*

Somewhere in the far corners of her mind, she had secretly hoped that the mention of Paris would stimulate Mark's natural romantic tendencies and somehow, some way, they would wind up in Paris for a super romantic interlude. But the idea of Paris didn't seem to faze him. She was left wondering if she should go. The City of Lights held such fond memories for her. The more she thought about it, the more it fed her image of the lonely-in-love woman in Paris, getting her cosmic house in order. When she mentioned the trip to Lois, Lois indeed confirmed that this time could be ideal because the stars suggested only good things coming from travel. Maybe it was time, Melanie pondered, for her to accept some of this astrology stuff after all.

The next thing she knew, she was perusing the Air France website, checking out flight schedules.

14

Several weeks had passed since the "cool it" e-mail from Mark. Melanie's life, as usual, was uneventful except for the daily drama at work.

Paris had been on her mind. It was a place that carried her thoughts back to her teenage years, when her parents had taken her to Paris. The City of Lights had made an impression on the romance-smitten fourteen year old. They had traveled to Paris on the luxury liner *Queen Mary,* one of the most fabulous modes of transportation at the time. Everywhere she had looked, romance was in the air. She treasured everything about it: the quaint and romantic cafés, the charm of St. Germain and Montparnasse, the boat rides on the Seine, and the lovers everywhere, strolling hand in hand.

Melanie had called Lois shortly after booking her flight for October 11. Her friend was a bit skeptical at first. "Why go to such a romantic place alone? Won't that be even more hurtful?"

"To some, I suppose; but the place re-ignites my belief in love."

Before long, Lois relented and joined in the excitement about the two-week trip.

Melanie's main problem was a cover story to Lenny. After much thought, she had a brainstorm and simply asked him to go with her. She had an inner sense of triumph when he did just what she predicted and begged off because of business reasons and not enough lead time. She thought, *Guess most of my senses about him are accurate.* It was a disappointing observation. He did say he'd take care of Schneider.

Lois drove her to the airport. Melanie wondered why her friend had a tear in her eye when they hugged goodbye. *Does Lois know something I don't?*

Melanie had psyched herself up for the long flight. She knew she would occupy her time thinking about everything. As she gazed out the window at the passing cumulus, she drifted through the backwater of her life. She mused about the two Parisian trips with her first husband, Richard. They visited Paris on their honeymoon, and it was everything she had ever dreamed of. That trip was the culmination of all her girlhood dreams about love and romance: an enormously romantic setting, an attentive new husband, a sensitive lover. Everything was right. But by the time they went back, twenty years later, the trip was a futile effort to renew the old flame. It was a dismal and disappointing trip, which put the finishing touches on their imminent divorce.

Then there was her marriage to Lenny. How could she have been so wrong? Was it a rebound thing? Did she rush to fill the empty part of her life? But was Mark the answer?

The flight was the way she liked air travel—smooth and boring. She cleared Customs and took a cab to the Pullman Paris Tour hotel on the Left Bank, a short walk from the famous Eiffel Tower.

In several ways, this trip was a milestone. It was extremely daring for her to travel so far alone. But never before did she have such a serious problem to think out. By coming to the City of Lights, she wasn't relying on her intelligence and logic for a solution. Rather, she was hoping her emotions would provide the answer.

Of course her first impulse after checking into the hotel was to e-mail Mark.

Mark,

I hope you are doing well, and that the family situation is improving. I am in Paris! Yes, Paris, France. I needed to do some soul searching, and I couldn't think of a better place than the city I love. I don't know what I will find here, or what conclusions I will bring back, but I am open to what the stars have planned for me.

Be well, and know that I am thinking about you.
Melanie

After a short nap, she woke up to a breathtaking sight: the Tower lit up at night. It was the reason why Paris was the City of Lights. She blinked away tears as she sat on her balcony, absorbing the beauty, so happy to be there.

Within a few days, Melanie established a routine. She visited the places that gave her the happiest and most romantic feelings of her life.

She ate almost exclusively at outdoor cafés and at one near her hotel in particular. There she'd have things she hadn't even thought of in years, such as goat cheese, boulette d'avesnes (a spicy cheese), and other delicacies. She rediscovered French coffees and lattes. Naturally, the time she spent in reverie was bittersweet, but she did a lot of fun things she had done before. She went shopping for sexy lingerie at Printemps. She marveled, *Who could have more sexy lingerie than the French?* Some of it even made her blush. She took riverboat rides on the batobus. She also made a special effort to have one super-elegant meal at a favorite place, Le Procope on Rue de l'Ancienne Comédie.

It was the fourth afternoon of the trip. She was at her usual café enjoying a new treat. She was so relaxed, that she even had a fond thought that she hoped Lenny was having a good day on the golf course. Absorbed in her thoughts and the superb latte, she suddenly noticed a shadow that fell over her, covering the early fall sunlight. She looked up to see a tall man standing beside her. In halting and heavily accented English he said, "Pardon me, Madame. I heard you speak English to the waiter and …" he gestured at the table, "noticing you are alone, I wondered if I might be so bold to join you in a demitasse?" He added, "I am always looking for ways to improve my terrible English. May I?" He gestured to the empty seat across from her.

Melanie was so startled that she almost automatically answered, "Of course."

He sat and gazed at her. It was her first chance to take him in. Besides being tall, he was slim and impeccably dressed. His long, silver hair swept back off his handsome, angular face. His teeth were as bright as his smile, which he flashed often.

He was so handsome and urbane, that her first instinct was to lower her head. But he didn't allow the awkward moment to last. He reached his hand across the little table and said, "I am Lyle Bishop. I am a professor of medieval architecture here at the Sorbonne."

Melanie could tell by his appearance and demeanor that if only half of what he said was true, he was an elegant gentleman—not one of the gigolos who prowled this part of Paris seeking rich older women. His complexion was so ruddy that he might have been an African big game hunter. It contrasted markedly with his silver hair and dazzling white teeth.

He broke off his gaze and started to engage her in conversation. "As you can see, English is a second language for me, and I am always looking to improve it. It's ironic, actually, because I am English by birth; but a lifetime in France has made me a Francophile and not a very good English speaker."

Melanie loosened up and smiled. "So you're looking for an English tutor, are you?"

He laughed. "Ah, you found me out. No matter how bad my English is, I am still a connoisseur of beauty, and yours cannot be ignored."

She didn't remember if she thanked him or not, but he was so witty and charming that soon she found herself agreeing to a date that he promised would include sightseeing. When he learned that she was not new to Paris he said, "Why don't you select the place to eat, and I will do my best to show you some of the architectural wonders of Paris."

Dressing carefully that night, Melanie selected an outfit that wasn't touristy. While its fashion was understated, it was more her style: romantic and enticing.

She selected a Left Bank restaurant called Au Bourguignon du Marais. It was on the Rue François Miron and was not hard for them to find. A small place, it had maybe ten or twelve tables. Although they could spot a few tourists, most of the patrons were French. The kitchen galley was behind the small bar. Melanie's French was good enough to chat with the owners, who were husband and wife.

Lyle seemed impressed with her worldly ways. He said, "At least let me order. I am beginning to feel like the tourist."

He had an easygoing manner, and it felt so natural to be lighthearted with him.

She asked, "Have you made our dinner selection?"

"Yes. I hope you like it. Appetizer first."

Melanie nodded and smiled.

"It's a jambon persille, a thinly sliced ham garnished with chopped endives," Lyle said.

"Wonderful," she replied. Melanie was beginning to suspect that his English was better than he had first led her to believe.

The main course was grilled beef filet, smothered with sautéed chanterelles, and a few green beans to dress the plate.

She applauded daintily, smiling.

Lyle's unique Anglo–Franco charm won people over quickly. The proprietors fussed over them so much that Melanie thought the other diners might feel slighted. When they left, there was only a bit of snap in the late fall air. They sauntered into a little square dominated by an equestrian bronze statue of a French military figure. Across the street, the patrons of a bistro poured into the street laughing. Their gaiety was contagious, and Melanie and Lyle reveled in it, squeezing their hands tightly together.

The Swatch store at the start of Cherche Midi was crammed with tourists; in contrast, behind it, the Camper store was busily serving Parisians. On Cherche Midi, black iron posts set at regular spaces at the edge of the sidewalk were an unmistakable reminder that they were in Paris. Little French cars were parked wherever their owners could fit them. Lyle said, "Now for a digestif and coffee at the Brasserie de L'île St-Louis."

From their café, with a view back across the bridge and down Rue Saint-Louis en L'île, they ordered Calvados. Later they went toward Notre Dame by way of Île Saint-Louis. Near Metro Mairie, they walked across Quai des Célestins to Pont Marie. After crossing the bridge, they strolled along Rue Des Deaux Ponts to where it intersects with Rue Saint-Louis, heading toward Notre Dame and following Rue Saint-Louis en L'île.

He steered her over Pont Saint-Louis. On the other side, they walked past Notre Dame and stopped at Pont Archêveché to admire the ancient cathedral lit in soft lights. They studied it wordlessly for a while.

Melanie finally said, "It takes your breath away, doesn't it?"

"Yes. It is different than other European cathedrals, is it not?"

"I'm Jewish, but I've always admired Christian cathedrals. Most of them are magnificent."

Lyle gazed at Notre Dame. "It was cutting-edge architecture when it was built back around 1160. It's more Gothic than Renaissance," he said with a bit of wonder in his voice.

Later they were quiet, contemplative, standing on the banks of the Seine, watching the twinkle of moonlight on the rippling dark water. A tourist boat, music blaring, came by and broke the serenity. When she turned back to him, he was gazing at her—something she caught him doing from time to time. She smiled. "Monsieur?" she said, her eyes inquisitive.

"Just taking you in. You're so beautiful. I have to ask myself: a beautiful American woman, alone in Paris. Why?"

She lowered her head. "It's a place that I am familiar with and holds some beautiful memories."

"And you wish to recapture them?"

"Something like that."

"Are you sure?"

"I'm not here on the prowl, if that's what you mean. I'm not really sure why I accepted your invitation. I am well aware of the French reputation to always 'Cherchez la femme.'"

He looked at the water. "I guess I can't blame you for being suspicious. A beautiful woman in Paris, alone, should be careful. You are probably here for the most obvious reasons. Maybe the same reason many come. Loneliness. Are you lonely?"

"If I say yes, would that mean that you think it's the signal to come on to me?"

He looked puzzled. "'Come on?' Madame?"

She grinned now. "You know." She made an expressive gesture, "L'amour?"

His eyes brightened. "Ah. I am not up with things American. So you are lonely?"

She lowered her eyes. "I don't think anyone lies about being lonely. Only I don't intend to seek male companionship because of it."

"I understand and admire you for it." Then grinning, he added, "Although I can't say that pleases me. I find you so beautiful."

"Is that a main requisite for you?"

"Comme ça?"

"Does a woman have to be beautiful to interest you?"

"Yes and no. I know it is … What do you call it? The word you took from us?" His face brightened. "Ah yes: a cliché. But whether it is a cliché or not, I understand and appreciate what is inside a person as much as what is outside."

She cocked her head and looked at him. "You know that's the 'right' thing to say, don't you?"

He grinned. "Probably it is, but that does not make my feeling less true."

She smiled at him. "You are the kind of guy that one doesn't mind giving the benefit of the doubt. But let's face it, that would take time to really learn, and I'm only going to be here another five days."

He smiled and said, "I'd hurry to impress you with my sincerity."

She hid a smirk, huddled into her wrap against the chilly fall evening, and said, "Let's go. I need my beauty rest."

When she again looked up, he had pressed his lips to hers. She responded almost instinctively, but quickly broke it off. "I'm sorry," she said, "but I'm not ready for anything."

"Anything?" he asked.

"Whatever you had in mind," she smiled.

"I'm sorry if I offended you. I just couldn't help myself. I'm enjoying myself so much with you. I promise I will not, again, offend." He batted his eyelashes sweetly.

She smiled at his awkward attempt to amend things. She, too, was enjoying his company and didn't want him to go away.

The next day they met in Saint German for breakfast and took in a day of browsing the myriad galleries, antique shops, and bookstores. The place that so fascinated the artists of the world had a hold on Melanie.

When Lyle brought her back to the hotel after an apéritif and late dinner, he again kissed her. This time it was a goodnight kiss, and she didn't resist but rather lingered a moment, herself caught up with his masculine aroma and sweet lips.

Alone in her room, she needed to catch her breath. She went to the balcony and looked out at Paris, then went to her computer. She had been disappointed that Mark had not written. In fact, it was one of the reasons why she accepted Lyle's invitations. Tonight, however, there was mail.

Babe

Guess what? I'm coming to Paris. Have to see a high-profile client. But I just have to see you, too! I'll get you details of my arrival. Can't wait.

Mark

Her heart leaped. Would this be the watershed, the miracle that would decide their future for them? Her pulse raced; his message had rocked her world.

She fought her pillow most of the night. The long night would not let her go, so near dawn she got up, poured herself a hotel-supplied latte, took it out on the balcony, and watched the sun rise over Paris. First a soft pastel pink lit up the eastern sky, then the sparkling sun appeared. Mark would be arriving tonight. Maybe the stars were right: Her life was about to change.

15

Melanie was more confused than ever. What happened to Mark's "family problem"? What happened to them "cooling it for a while"? She needed someone to talk to about it, and she immediately thought of Lyle. Luckily, he wasn't teaching and agreed to meet her at their café. As soon as she had called him, she began to wonder why. After all, wasn't it just a friendship of a few days? She hardly knew him, yet she was about to trust him for advice on the most important relationship in her life. As she waited for him, she realized why. Although the friendship was just beginning, she sensed that the handsome Parisian embodied the spirit and allure of his city. The essential emotions that made this city the capital of everything romantic were part of him. Further, he had an introspective, meditative character, probably due to his passion for history. She wished she could develop that kind of calm. His presence gave her a comfortable sense of security.

Tense, she was already through her first café creme when he arrived. She saw that he was wearing woolen slacks, an expensive polo shirt, Italian leather loafers, and a sweater. He was the type of polished Parisian who looked sharp even in casual clothes. Her anxiety must have shown on her face as he leveled his gaze at her. "What is it, Melanie?"

She lowered her eyes a bit. "I've been thrown a curve. Mark is arriving in Paris today and wants to see me. I want to see him, but I am deathly afraid of the outcome. Is it a final goodbye, or is it another step on this unpredictable journey? I came here to figure things out on my own, but now everything has become complicated."

His latte arrived, and he stirred sugar into it as he pondered her dilemma.

"Well Melanie, those are good questions. But you really can't answer them yourself. You try to fill in the blanks, and what usually happens to you? You get it wrong, and then you act it out with consequences. What do you hope will happen here today in the City of Love?"

Melanie sighed deeply. "Lyle, did you have to remind me of the romance this city exudes? I know that all too well. It's the very reason I am here, to capture the spirit of romance and then put it all in the proper perspective. But I am scared. To see him will undoubtedly heighten my feelings." She blushed a bit. "With Paris as the backdrop, loving him cannot be anything but pure ecstasy, and then what? Another let down? This one would be unforgettable. I'm so confused."

"Honey, you know how the world works. Life is not planned, nor does it always have a justification for its course. Feelings ebb and flow in the environment. This city will add flavor to your situation, but it is not responsible for the direction of the relationship. You cannot control things, as I know you would like to. For you, it is better to stay grounded and concentrate on why you are here and what you planned to achieve from this trip. After all, it really is about your life, isn't it?"

As they sipped their café creme and nibbled on a goat cheese salad, Melanie was impressed with all of Lyle's brilliance and ability to capture concepts she couldn't see just yet. He was right that she couldn't control things. She thanked him for his ideas and opted to take a walk around the little neighborhood of the Tower she so loved. She could never get enough of this city, never.

He said, "My favorite part of town. Could I join you?"

"Of course. How could I turn down an offer from such a handsome gentleman?"

As she slipped her arm through his, she thought, *He is quite a catch. A lot of women would fall right into his arms. While I don't need another wrinkle in this romance with Mark, I have to understand, too, that Mark isn't the only man I could be happy with. Is that what this trip is all about—to let me know that there could be others?* As they were on their way back to her hotel, her cell phone chirped. Her heart lurched. Lyle's peripheral glance was on her as she answered. It was Mark. "Mel, bonjour. I'm here. I'm at my hotel. How are you?"

"Fine, Mark. Glad you arrived safely. This certainly is a surprise."

"Yes, and I'm glad it happened this way. I have been wanting you and missing you. Can we have dinner tonight? I can get us into the Jules Verne at the Eiffel Tower if you want. It usually takes two months to get a reservation; but my Paris client is a bigshot, and he can do it. If you've never been, it's a must for a Paris visit. I can pick you up at your hotel."

"Mark, that would be great. What time should I be ready?"

"I'll pick you up at eight. How's that?"

"Fine. See you then." That's how the conversations were with Mark, short and purposeful.

Lyle was wearing a kind of Cheshire grin when she looked at him.

He said, "I hope you get everything you wish for tonight. I watched your expression as you were talking to Mark, and it was quite evident that this man really has a hold on you. I see your love and your passion for him. Just be careful that you don't let it take all your wonderful self-worth away that you have come to Paris to regain. You are working hard to reclaim Melanie and go forward in your transformation. You know how to reach me." He brushed her lips with his and was off.

As she sat on her hotel balcony, Melanie thought about what he had said. She was looking at the Tower that she loved, so close she could feel its presence. One of the last butterflies of the fall season fluttered toward her and settled on the wrought iron balcony railing. For a moment, the beauty of its black and orange wingspan mesmerized her. It stood perfectly still, as if it belonged there.

A butterfly knows what change is all about, she pondered. This tiny creature actually is born twice. In its new physical structure, it forms a spare set of embryonic cells. *Perhaps the butterfly is a reminder that I, too, can be reborn and have a spiritual renaissance. Maybe that's my fate.* She recalled the old Chinese proverb says that if your lover leaves you, and a butterfly settles itself near you, then your love is bound to return one day. It was a fanciful idea, but she saw the butterfly as just that: A renewal of love.

She picked out the perfect dress, and did her hair just how Mark liked it. While waiting for him she was anxious, wondering why he suddenly would go halfway around the world to see her. Especially because he was the one who had put things on hold. After looking over the final touches of her makeup, she headed for the lobby to endure an anxious wait.

When she spotted him coming toward her from the front entrance, she lit up. He was as handsome as ever. He fit right in with the elegant marble and brass opulence of the hotel lobby. He swept her into his arms. "You take my breath away. I'm so happy to see you. I've missed you. And now we are together, here in your city of love. It's nothing short of otherworldly."

"I've missed you, too. It's funny that we ended up here together. Don't you want to know why I'm here?" she asked.

"Aren't you curious?" He had to take a step back to see her; he had been holding her that closely.

"Yes, I want to know. But not right away. I need you so much, that I want to savor this moment."

She was in his arms, her lips close to his ear. She murmured a response, afraid that she would go overboard in expressing her joy. He took her hand and headed for the front door. She stopped abruptly at the front door and tugged him toward the elevator.

Minutes later they were in her room. When their bare skin touched, the shock was electric. She had no intention to be subtle. Her lips were on his, their tongues plunging, before she could even finish unbuttoning his shirt. They didn't make it to the bed, but dropped as one to the deep rug. Breathlessly, they continued to remove layer after layer of what separated them from pure flesh. The room quivered like an earthquake as they joined together lustily, culminating in a crazed, explosive release that was nearly simultaneous. Her head on his shoulder, she listened to his heart beat until sleep consumed them.

Finally, Melanie returned to reality and remembered they had a reservation for dinner. Knowing they were going to be late, Mark made a quick phone call. When he hung up, he assured Melanie that their table would still be waiting for them. She was impressed with his take-charge approach and how he seemed always to know the right things to say.

As her hotel was just around the corner from the Eiffel Tower, walking was the only way to go. What a backdrop for a kiss: the glittering Eiffel Tower! Melanie was speechless, never having dreamed that she would be in the city of love with the love of her life.

Melanie was a sophisticated traveler. Still, she gaped like a country bumpkin at the grandeur of the Jules Verne restaurant. It was elegant yet uniquely modern. At the one hundred twenty-five–meter level on the Eiffel Tower, the last glow of sunset was breathtaking. At their window-side table, they sipped their before-dinner cocktails as the lights of the city came on. Below, the city was a panoramic wonderland, framed by the lattice ironwork of the Eiffel's structure, parts of which could be seen from the windows. While French cuisine can be heavy, they ordered light fish dishes, so when they were done with dinner, they felt relaxed.

Their conversation ran all over the place. Melanie told Mark why she had come to Paris and what she had hoped to achieve. She explained how she was transforming like a butterfly, right before her eyes, doing things she never imagined she would. For so long, it seemed as if life had her cornered. But now she had more courage, and life was expanding.

Mark listened carefully and nodded. "So then," he said, lifting up her hand for a kiss. "You have found yourself in uncharted waters. Come on, I love the merry-go-round by the river. I've been thinking about it all day and thinking of you on it."

She smiled and said, "Yes, la tour de ménage." It was a short walk in the crisp, fall air.

Melanie couldn't help smiling and laughing like a schoolgirl as they whirled around on the ménage. The horses were painted in a colorful yet stylish manner that didn't seem childish, the way they did in the States. She thought, *Leave it to the French to infuse a sense of artistic sophistication, even when it came to merry-go-round horses.* The music, too, was noticeably different. In America, carnival ride music is whirly burly, honky tonk. But the one they rode featured a Parisian waltz, played with bells.

After this fantasy ride, Mark then whisked her off to the batobus, several steps down from the carousel. This night, all the people aboard, from tourists to old French couples, were lovers as they glided along the shimmering Seine. The lights from the Tower could be seen reverberating off the buildings, and the entire city was lit up. The wind was soft, and they held each other close, feeling and hearing only their silent words, something Melanie was sure she would never forget, as she painted the picture in her mind. When they disembarked, they walked arm in arm up to Pont des Arts, considered the most romantic bridge in Paris.

"What is that on the other side?" she asked.

He smiled. "Don't you recognize La Louvre?"

"Oh," she said. "It's so different at night."

Mark said, "You know how lovers declare their eternal love here?"

"How?"

"They write their names on a padlock and lock it to the bridge."

She smiled and gazed at him, "How romantic!"

"So I'm going to write our names right here."

"You are?" she said in disbelief. "Using what?"

He reached into his pocket and took out a small key and padlock. "With this," he said, grinning. He showed her that he had engraved their names upon it, and then he locked it to a portion of the iron railing, keeping a watchful eye out for the gendarme. As he did so, he tossed the key into the Seine River and said, "I confess my undying love for you!"

They giggled like a couple of teenagers as they hurried away from the scene of their crime.

Once back at her hotel, he began kissing her in the empty elevator; and when the door opened at the correct floor before they realized it, they were glad to see nobody waiting for the elevator.

In the middle of the night they found that that god of love had more plans for them. Later Melanie arose, wrapped her robe around her, and went to the balcony to watch the sun come up over Paris.

The first hint was a pink blush, which outlined a church spire on the bank of the river. Mark approached her quietly, wrapped his arms around her waist, and nestled his chin into her shoulder. He nibbled on her ear and basked in the scent of her hair.

He said, "I saw something at the Jules Verne that said, "A moment spent at the Jules Verne will remain forever engraved in the mind of the person who lives it."

"It was a fabulous view," she murmured.

"But I think that every moment spent here with you will remain with me forever." She turned, sought his eyes in the dim light, kissed him, and said, "I will never forget how wonderful you have been tonight."

16

In the quiet of morning, they sipped coffee on the balcony. Both were deep in thought as they overlooked Paris. The sun had been up for a while, and the air was comfortably warm. The Tower loomed nearby, reminding them that they weren't just anywhere in the world. She knew he would be leaving for work soon. Not wanting to end on a negative note, Melanie chose not to query Mark about his family problems. The situation that presumably was keeping them apart was foremost on her mind, but she held a tight rein on it. She would leave it to him whether or not he wanted to discuss his son's problems.

He was first to speak. His tone was rather anxious when he asked, "You know how much I love you, don't you?"

She was hesitant. "I think so. But due to your family's focus right now, I did not expect to see you for a while."

He cocked his head and waited.

She said, "You send me such mixed signals. I came here alone, to sort out my feelings, and suddenly you appear. Surely you know by now how much I am drawn to you. I can't resist you."

He lowered his head. When he raised his eyes to meet hers, he was earnest. "I want you desperately. I always have, since high school."

He got up and paced a bit before sitting back down.

"Back then, I imagined that you would turn me down. I made assumptions about how society saw me. As a result, I turned away from what I wanted. I dove into my studies and worked three times harder than anyone else. I ended up achieving the success that I have today."

"Your success is phenomenal," Melanie said.

"Thanks."

There was silence for a few moments, and then Mark continued.

"When I met Susan, it dawned on me how wrong my assumptions were. She was patient and accepted me. I learned two crucial things that year. First, that people filter life through their own experience. Second, that people process events in a vacuum, making assumptions about others' behavior without being in their own unique mindset. These two discoveries were liberating."

"You realized that you need not have separated yourself from everyone at school."

"Yes, you're right. So all these years later, when I found myself so close to a divorce, you suddenly pop up on the horizon. I've never cheated before in my marriage, but I want you more than anything. Both of us are married to other people. So we're both in a difficult position. If you will have me as I am able to give of myself, maybe we can be together for a while. A long-term commitment is not in the cards for me. Not right now."

Her heart thudded to the pit of her stomach. *Why did I see him again? Why didn't I ask him right off about his intentions? Clearly he is confused; and now I am, too.*

"You are devoted to your family. That's understandable. But I, selfishly, want to be with you. I have grown children, too. I don't expect you to give up your children. But I do want to make a life with you. If that's not where we're headed, then my dream for us is history."

He turned his face away, unable to bear looking in her eyes.

Melanie continued, "What I am learning from my soul-searching and the time spent with you is how tough it is to feel unconditional love for another adult. It is not easy to love without expectations."

She stared at Paris for a moment. "I came to this city so that it could tell me something that I needed to hear. It has whispered a truth to me since I first arrived, and this morning I allowed myself to listen. When you love someone, you must give them the freedom to be," Melanie told Mark tenderly. "I'm not going to insist on anything. You must choose for yourself, just as I must also choose. So remember that although I'm available now, I might not always be."

His face filled with emotion. "Thank you," he said, clasping her hand. "That's beautiful and honest, so like you." He let go of her hand and turned to leave. Without facing her, he said, "I have to meet a client. We'll talk soon."

She was crying before the door closed. Abruptly, she felt alone. *How could that be?* she asked herself. *Here I am in Paris, carrying on a beautiful relationship—flawed as it is, but filled with emotion and romance. Why do I feel sad, as if I'm the only person in the world?*

For a few hours, she cried a bit, thumbed through a French fashion magazine, and dozed a little. When the phone rang, her heart leaped. *Is it Mark, with good news for them?* She hurried to pick up. It was Lyle.

"Mel? Is this a bad time? I had a premonition that you needed me."

She burst out, "Lyle! How did you know?"

"Didn't I ever tell you I was psychic?" he kidded. "How about a promenade around the Tower? Then maybe a latte?"

She wiped away her tears. "For you, dear, of course. Meet me at twelve—midi—at Les Deux Magots."

"Love it. See you then."

As usual, Lyle was late; but not very much, just fashionably so. He was worth waiting for. When he saw her, he threw a strong arm around her and said, "You look so intense. And I'm not sure what else."

She couldn't hide her sadness, and her face showed it. As they strolled toward Les Deux Magots, Lyle's strong arm made her feel immediately better. She had a fleeting thought, *Is it is curse to love men so much?*

Now it was Mel, giving the Lyle some French history. She said, "I'm sure you know that this place was big with a lot of artists: Elsa Triolet, André Gide, Jean Giraudoux, and Picasso."

He smiled. "Not to mention Fernand Léger, Prévert, Sartre, and old Papa Hemingway."

"The feeling of great things just permeates the place," she said in awe. She was feeling Paris deeply. It had crept into her heart. It was a place synonymous with l'amour. *Everyone wants to be in love here,* she thought. They continued their stroll to Saint-Germain des Prés. It was a special part of Paris for Melanie. She wished she could come back with her dog, Schneider, and spend several months here. Drink it all in. Be French every day.

As they stirred their cafés she suddenly said, "I'm so in love with him. But it is going nowhere," she sighed. "I want a soul mate, not someone who pops in and out of my life." She gestured west. "Perhaps I should go back to my normal life at home and consider Mark a luxury now and then. He came into my life for a reason, to give me the courage to expand my horizons. Then he leaves me to continue the work he started. Maybe I'm not supposed to end up with my soul mate, just benefit from his brief interludes in my life."

Lyle pondered what she had said. When he finally answered, he said, "That is one way to look at it. If only I had sage advice to offer. But alas, I do not, other than the age-old adage, to follow your heart."

She smiled, and there was an awkward moment of silence. Lyle then said, "I have so enjoyed our friendship. I'm sad that that your trip is coming to an end. I hope that we meet again. Who knows where our paths will cross? Maybe the next time we meet, we will both be single and open to each other in a different way. But for now, I am content for the time we have. I know I didn't tell you much about my own relationship quandary. It seemed so small next to yours."

Melanie was taken aback. Here was a good friend who had his own romantic quandary that she had no clue about. She reached across the table and took his hand. "Lyle, I am so sorry. This talking about me all the time gets old, doesn't it? Do you feel you know me well enough to tell me about it?"

He gazed at her. "One of my problems is I'm a very private person, and I would be embarrassed telling you about it."

Now Melanie looked hurt. "I thought we were friends. New friends—but good friends, nonetheless."

He sipped some café. His eyes searched hers for trust. "A while back, I fell in love with a much younger woman."

Melanie smiled. "Isn't that a universal thing? Don't all dashing older men, such as yourself, fall for young women?"

Lyle didn't smile. Quickly, she added, "Lyle, I'm sorry, please don't think I'm making light of your problem. You've been so supportive of me. It's just that I expect a man like you to fall for a younger woman."

"Why?" he said.

"You have so much to offer, and you're so good looking."

"I am feeling close to you, and I have a need to tell you. You see, I guess it's the thing I'm leaving out. It's not only that she is young—it's that I've never been in love before. Yes, I live in Paris, whose very name is synonymous with love. Yet I've never been in love, not really. Maybe I thought I had been in the past, but not like this."

"That sounds wonderful for you, to have found such a love. What's the problem, then?"

"The problem is…." He looked uncomfortable. "She's not in love with me."

Melanie wanted to reach over and hold him. But instead she said, "I'm sorry. You're so charming. Just let me be your best friend, then. Someone who thinks you are wonderful. My friendship could be some comfort to you."

He flashed his best smile. "It does, Melanie. Believe me, it does."

Something about him made her feel that she owed him more of herself, of her time, of her compassion. She said, "I'm going home at the end of the week, and I wish we could spend more time together."

His features brightened. "Maybe we can. I'm visiting London for an errand. Would you care to join me?"

This was so unexpected that she was taken aback. But Melanie quickly realized it was a superb idea. She said simply, "Yes, I'd like that."

"Merveilleux!" he exclaimed. "Pack your things, and I'll pick you up in the morning. We'll catch the eight o'clock Eurostar."

Not having been to London, this trip was a treat for Melanie. Excited about the chance to travel on European trains, she found herself able to put the problem with Mark on the back burner. The high-speed trains were cutting-edge technology, and she had heard they were very comfortable. The two had breakfast on the train in a very comfortable compartment and watched the French countryside glide by in a passing panorama of flat farmland. Toward the end of the trek was the passage through the Chunnel, the tunnel under the English Channel between France and England. Twenty or so minutes later, they were surrounded by English countryside.

They were in London in time for lunch. Just like a kid, Lyle was eager to show her everything. Melanie had always thought of England as a tranquil place. But not London, she soon learned. She marveled at the hustle and bustle, the busyness of the city. And the diversity! People wore every kind of head gear, ranging from the scally cap, to the hijab, to the turban. Oxford street was very different from the Champs-Élysées; and English was spoken everywhere, a delightful departure from her trying to make her French sound passable. They took a London cab to a small restaurant that Lyle was familiar with on the Thames River. They had a view of the busy river traffic while they lunched on fish and chips, washed down with a dark lager beer.

Lyle said, "The best way to see the most of London in a short time is a river cruise on the Thames."

After lunch they boarded a luxurious river cruise boat for the trip up the river. The tour guide pointed it all out: Big Ben, the famous London Bridge, the historic warship anchored in the river, as well as many other sights, including the famous London Eye. The Eye, the tallest ferris wheel in Europe, afforded an outstanding view of the city. Petrified of its majestic height, she declined the offer to sample this wonder..

They found a nice place for a traditional afternoon tea. During a lull in the conversation, Melanie approached the subject of Lyle's relationship problem. "So, tell me more about your paramour."

Lyle hesitated. She saw it wasn't easy for him. "She's a lovely girl, really. A bio scientist, yet not the nerdy, scientist type. She is beautiful. As amazing as she is outside, she is even more amazing inside. A truly humanitarian person, she genuinely cares about others."

Melanie let that sink in. She realized how often she was accustomed to think of beauty as external. Suddenly she felt very shallow. She had to say, "She sounds like a wonderful person."

"She is. And I'm afraid I'm crazy about her."

"What do you mean, 'afraid'?"

He sighed. "As I said, I love her. But to her, I am just a dear, dear friend." He paused. "Don't get me wrong. She would do anything for me. And she has. But…." His voice lapsed sad. "She doesn't love me the way I want and need."

Melanie said, "That's got to hurt."

"No worse pain than unrequited love, my dear. None."

He quickly brightened. "Look, I didn't take you to London to cry in my beer with me. Next stop: Buckingham Palace and the changing of the guard."

With that announcement, they were off. This event was truly a treat. The pomp and circumstance was over the top, not to mention the perfect symmetry of British Army guards executing their practiced drill in the actual changing of the guard. The troops were resplendent in their brilliant red uniforms and renowned black-beaver hats. Lyle took a picture of her hugging the arm of a stiff-lipped, stoic Palace guard who would not smile or acknowledge her if his life were at stake.

Next they visited St. Paul's Cathedral, which, according to the tour guide, "Embodies the spiritual life and heritage of the British people." It was magnificent. Started during the Reformation, it had many features, Catholic as well as Protestant Church of England.

The hotel that Lyle selected was the Thistle Picadilly, a truly Victorian structure near Leicester Square. They had adjoining rooms at the hotel, and both looked forward to a nap before dinner. When Lyle tapped at her door, she was just waking. He waited while she went into the bathroom to get ready.

They walked to a nearby restaurant, and Melanie selected the shepherd's pie. She could not finish, it was so filling. "Delicious," she said. "But so different from the French cuisine."

"True," Lyle said, "I have to adjust my taste buds when I make a trip back to my roots."

This time it was Lyle who brought up his problem again. He said, "Daphne is English, too, but she has a job in research at the Sorbonne."

"Has someone else come between you?" Melanie asked.

He lowered his eyes. She detected a small frown. "Yes, actually. She met someone else, and I know she is beginning to favor him more and me less."

"That's sad."

"Ah," he said philosophically, "but it is the way of love. The one you love does not always love you back."

"Wouldn't it be best to move on? Try to forget her?"

"Yes, it most definitely would, but the heart is stubborn. It does not want to give up that which it loves so much."

"That certainly rings home for me," Melanie said, reaching for his hand. When she saw how unhappy talking about it made him, she decided she would not broach the subject again. Better to make him happy and enjoy their time together, especially because she had no idea how to advise him.

The next day, they took the train to Stonehenge. Even today, the three-thousand-year-old rock formation remains an enigma. Lyle was highly knowledgeable about it, and filled her in on the history, which she found fascinating.

They spent a more relaxing day in the English countryside, where they lingered over every meal and especially afternoon tea. They spent their last night in a quaint English bed and breakfast, and the next day they headed for Heathrow Airport for Melanie's flight home. They hugged tightly at the airport, and she momentarily clung to him. Her lips brushed his, and she murmured, "Will we see each other again?"

"I very much hope so. Dash me off an e-mail when you get home. I'll need to know you got home safely."

She had a lot to think about on the long flight home. She wondered, *Is this someone new in my romantic life? Or is he just a dear friend?* She asked herself a series of questions. *What do I want him to be to me? He's single and free. If I were lovers with Lyle, I wouldn't be in the same situation that I am in with Mark. And Lyle's so nice, so charming. But there has to be more—more of which maybe Lois could fill in for me.* Melanie was deep in thought.

She was dozing when the little chirp of rubber and a heavy thump let her know the plane had landed, and that she was home from her European adventure.

17

She felt so changed, that it was as if she had been away for months. In a few weeks it would be her birthday, and instead of feeling older, she was feeling like a teenager. She wondered if Lenny would notice when she returned. She stepped back into reality and headed toward the baggage claim. Of course customs would be "fun" and would only make the re-entry back home more laborious.

Finally she was settled into her convertible and was on her way back to her house. She breathed a sigh of relief. Had this trip been worth it? Not in ways she had expected; she had gained a new dear friend and a memory of the most romantic evening of her life.

Could she go back to living the life she'd left behind? She hesitated before opening her front door. She sensed that something was not the same. She noticed a tiny sticky note stuck to the front door jamb. She peered at it and read aloud, "Welcome Home, Honey." *What is this?* she wondered. *Am I at the wrong house? Or had the usually oblivious Lenny had an epiphany?* Before she could shuffle her bags inside, Lenny emerged from the door and was beside her, hugging her and kissing her, something he had not done in years. His excitement over her return seemed genuine, so she was puzzled.

"I missed you," he said fervently. "Wow, you look great. You look a whole lot younger. I guess this trip did you well."

"I missed you, too," she said.

Nuzzling her ear, he murmured, "Why don't you go and settle in, and then we can have dinner together. You can tell me all about it."

She was aghast. *Tell him all about it? Wouldn't that be something!* And whereas she had never felt much guilt before regarding her husband, that comment did tweak her conscience. What kind of drama had she created? Mark, Lyle, and now Lenny. Trying to explain all that was the last thing she wanted to do.

When she was finally settled in and Schneider had expended all his energy slobbering her and dancing around, Lenny took her hand. "I made a reservation at your favorite restaurant."

"That's so nice, honey."

He said hesitantly, "I know what you're thinking. Who am I, a re-packaged Lenny?"

She chuckled. "Yeah, I was kind of wondering."

He lowered his eyes. "I have to admit that I have missed you. I've been thinking what we are all about, and maybe where we were going."

Talking about his feelings was truly uncharacteristic of Lenny. Perhaps in her absence, he had been replaced by an alien Lenny? Her curiosity was piqued.

"I was thinking what it was like when we first were married," he explained. "How we couldn't wait to be alone and together."

This was a sad statement, and the raw truth was more than she was prepared to hear. She gazed intently at him and answered simply, "Yes."

"I know it isn't like that anymore," he said, "and I miss it. I missed you on this trip."

Melanie was at a loss for words. "I—"

He cut her off. "I know you're confused. I am, too." He took her into his arms and kissed her. The kiss was so passionate, and she had loved him once, so she couldn't help but respond. She had been caught off-guard. Now she struggled with tangled, odd feelings.

Still holding her, he said, "After your last trip to New York and Massachusetts, I was intensely lonely. And this time, I found myself wandering around the house, missing you desperately. But it is more than just that. It is something else."

"What's that?"

"At first I couldn't put my finger on it. Then I realized that lately you've been more like we were at the beginning of our relationship. There's a sparkle in your eye. A mischievous, teasing allure about you that makes me want to jump your bones. You seem more alive, more assertive. You have new confidence, definitely a new you. I guess I want to be a new me, too, to show you that I can be like that."

For the rest of the night, Melanie had to face some new facts. *Was this what I wanted all along, for my husband to once again be my lover?* She suspected that Lenny's change of heart was due to loneliness, and that his new personality was probably not lasting. *I'm not prepared for this,* she kept saying over to herself. *Does Lenny still love me? Is the attention and newfound love from Lenny too late, or can I recapture the loving feeling for him again? Having been in a quasi-platonic relationship with Lenny for so long, intimacy seems … unsettling. What will happen? Was there something about how I acted that contributed to us drifting apart?*

He was grinning when he said, "Ya know, I had to suppress a sudden urge to hop on a plane and go over there and join you. But of course I knew you wanted to be alone to relive some stuff."

Her fingers went to her hair, and she began anxiously twirling a curl. *Oh my gosh!* she thought. *Wouldn't that have been something, maneuvering the three of them around Paris without meeting each other, without a blunder?* Suddenly she realized what dangerous chess she was playing, and that in the game of adultery, she might be over her head. It wasn't any longer just about her own future.

It was all so bewildering. She could be starring in a TV soap opera. All she knew for sure was that she had jet lag and could barely deal with Lenny over dinner at the restaurant.

When Melanie got on the phone with Lois the next day, Melanie was eager to spill the beans about everything. Further, Melanie learned, Lois had news to share, too. They met for drinks at Lois's house.

Sitting poolside with a pitcher of Margaritas, Melanie couldn't contain her curiosity. "What? What is it?" she asked. "What did I miss?"

"You missed the Bacchus Bash for the historical society," Lois said, tossing her blonde hair for dramatic effect.

"You're right," Melanie said. "That was certainly bad timing on my part. I bet they had some fabulous wines, as always."

"Yep," Lois reported. "*Everyone* was there, and asked where you were. But the best part was the auction. My husband bid like a crazy man and won us a river cruise."

"What river? Remember, there are alligators in Florida."

"The Yangtze, in China!" Lois revealed excitedly. "We will visit the Great Wall, the Forbidden City, and the see the once-buried sculptures of the terracotta warrior army."

"Geez, talk about a change of scenery! We've got to look into the Chinese weather and do some clothes shopping for you."

"Yes, preparing is a bit overwhelming! How did your trip turn out? Was Paris fabulous?"

"You're not going to believe who showed up from California."

Lois's eyes got big. Her jaw went slack. "No!"

"Actually, yes!"

"How did it go?" Lois asked tentatively.

"Oh, more fabulous than fabulous," said Melanie, gesturing expansively. "I had the most romantic evening of my entire life. And I'm more confused than ever."

She went on to tell how she and Mark practically floated on air around Paris. When Melanie finally told Lois about Mark's incredibly romantic gesture on the bridge, Lois said, "Stop it, you're making me hope to bump into Bolo Yeung when I'm on my trip."

"Lois, your obsession with martial arts movies has me worried. Doesn't he play the villain?"

"Yes, but villains need to look tough, hence the great body."

Melanie's giggle was nervous, and Lois could see something was up, so she let her friend have the floor. Melanie started, "Not only was Paris wonderful, but also I met another man, a charming Englishman, Lyle, who lives in Paris. We took a trip together to London, and he was a wonderful companion."

Lois's jaw dropped. "Wow, girl, when you have an affair, you really go over the top. I'm a bit jealous." She saw that Melanie didn't want to crow about Lyle, but that she was truly troubled. Lois said, "I can see your dilemma."

Melanie rolled her eyes. "You haven't heard the end of it."

Lois peered directly at her friend. "You did it with Lyle?"

"No, of course not. He was a gentleman, and I set limits. What Lyle and I had was purely platonic. But," she hesitated, "it definitely has the potential for romance if I say the word."

Lois leaned forward on her elbows, eyes bright. "Tell me about this intriguing character."

"I will. But first, something even more startling."

Lois said, "Not another man? Who?"

"It's *Lenny*. Can you believe that? When it rains, it pours. When I came home, he was happier to see me than Schneider. He had a welcome note on the door jamb written on a two-by-three yellow sticky. It was so cute that I'm always keeping it. He told me he missed me. He took me out to dinner at my favorite restaurant and wanted to know every detail. I did tell him about Lyle, but everything else had to stay under wraps."

"What the …" Lois said, stunned.

"And what's even more unbelievable—he wanted to make love to me last night. I was so torn, because my heart is somewhere else. But how could I say no to my husband? We had been apart for two weeks, and he wanted to make love to his wife."

Lois let out a long sigh. "Unbelievable. Men!"

"I know."

"So, did you?"

Melanie twisted some hair and nodded. "What else could I do? And believe it or not, I felt guilty because of Mark—even though Mark left me with no commitment. Maybe he's still sleeping with Susan; I have no idea. I have never been in more than one physical relationship at a time. I am sure the planets can't be the cause, or can they?"

With that question unanswered, silence filled the afternoon, punctuated only by the exotic whistle of a spot-breasted oriole. The sun's reflection sparkled on the aqua water of the pool. Both women sipped at their drinks.

Finally Melanie turned to her friend. "I know you want to ask, but are too much a lady—but yes. It was good. Not like Mark, but uniquely Lenny."

After a while Lois said, "Wow. This is really a pickle, isn't it? I think I need to look closely at the transits, and see what I might be missing. By the way, do you have any impulses, any initial feelings?"

"Yes," Mel said. "I'm so confused I want to run away from the world."

"You just did that. Can't do that again. No, you've got to figure this out and confront the situation. Obviously you can't have a life with two or three men."

"I know," Melanie said. "To tell you the truth, I'm looking forward to going to work tomorrow. Saving lives seems less stressful."

"I don't blame you."

Indeed, the next day, her job did turn out to be downright therapeutic. It was another busy day on the cardio ward, and she was soon buried in her work. She even forgot to check her e-mail. Later that night, as she put her weary feet up on the hassock and checked her e-mail, she found nothing from Mark. That was unusual, but she was too tired to worry about it.

As for Lenny, it was like coming home from work to a stranger. When she had opened the door, there he was, smiling quizzically, one hand behind his back. Then he presented her with a small gift of jewelry, which was really a surprise. He even decided how they would spend their evening: scrabble, her favorite, followed by actually going to bed at the same time. It seemed like the only thing that was left of the original Lenny was that when he went to bed, he slept like a dead man. A hurricane hitting the house couldn't wake him. This gave Melanie the privacy and the opportunity to respond to an e-mail from Lyle. She told him everything that had happened, and in closing, Melanie said that she didn't expect any advice because this was entirely too complicated.

Frankly, Mel wished she was the one giving advice to Lyle about his love life. She fully intended that the next e-mail would be all about him. She didn't want to have a one-sided relationship with anyone, especially someone she called a friend. Before she drifted off to sleep, she was wondering about this need to help others. She used to feel that way strongly, and not just because of her job; but as the years went by, it seemed that she had lost the energy and the drive. Now that she felt renewed, her interest in helping others had been reawakened, which made her feel more connected with the world. There was no feeling in the world that could compete with knowing that you are both needed and appreciated. Is this why Mark was in her world, to continue to unravel every layer of her, until she could grasp life with inner happiness and purpose? If so, the road was challenging and surprising every step of the way. Could there be more?

18

In the two weeks since Melanie had been home from Paris, she had sent Mark two e-mails but had not heard back from him. As usual, she worried constantly, her anxiety becoming negative. She knew this was not emotionally healthy, and she dove into her work to regain balance. She got very involved in a new case. The patient was a woman who had none of the usual risks for heart problems. She was slim and in her early thirties. As a runner, she was fit, and her blood tests showed no cholesterol or diabetes problems. Because her heart problems were stumping the doctors, the woman became quite depressed. Her name was Stephanie, and she had two kids.

One afternoon Melanie was checking Stephanie's chart. The patient had been dozing, but before Melanie was done, she awakened. Melanie was cheerful, as her job required.

"Hi, Stephanie. How are you today? I heard your daughter was going to be visiting you today?"

The young woman's voice was low. "Oh, yeah. I guess I forgot."

Melanie pretended to busy herself with chores in the room as she talked. "The desk nurse told me that she was here last week, and that she's a beautiful young lady."

Stephanie's face brightened a bit. "Oh, yeah. She's that."

"What does she like to do? Does she have any hobbies?"

Stephanie said, "She's into ballet."

"I love dance," said Melanie. "My daughter took lessons when she was a kid. I remember many of the recitals, and the cute costumes she wore. What's your daughter's name?"

"It's Bonnie."

"Pretty name. What time will she be here?"

Stephanie looked at her watch. "Oh shoot. She'll be here in a couple of hours. I was thinking of washing my hair."

"Sounds great. The doctor doesn't want you to be straining yourself, so why don't I send in one of the Candy Stripers to do it for you?"

Stephanie's eyes lowered. "Damn. I hate being an invalid."

Melanie approached the bed and gazed at her. "You're no invalid. I've seen your records. You're in very good shape."

"Tell that to my heart."

"The doctors are working on that. I hear they are closing in on an answer. It has something to do with a chemical imbalance. Nothing we can't fix."

Stephanie seemed to perk up. Melanie said, "You have a nice visit with your daughter, and I'll see you in the morning. Maybe we'll have some good news on your prognosis."

When she left the room, the young woman was visibly cheerier. It was interactions like these where Melanie found her significance. Although the medical part of her job was important, it was being able to brighten a patient's world with conversation and caring that gave Melanie what she really craved: to make a difference in someone else's life. It also allowed her to leave her troubles behind for brief interludes.

When she got home, of course, the languishing affair again got the best of her. She decided to send another e-mail.

Mark,

It's been a while since I've heard from you. My first question is, of course, are you okay? You know how my mind works. If you are, I am glad but can't help wondering if the family situation with your son has resolved or taken a turn for the worse.

I am still madly in love with you. I remember every detail of our glorious rendezvous in Paris. Please let me know how you are.

Mel

Melanie's kids were coming for her birthday. She was looking forward to seeing them and Ali.

She daydreamed about how wonderful life would be, shared with Mark. But Lenny was doing pretty well these days as a mate. He was continuing his hot pursuit of her, and she had a hard time adjusting to this shined-up husband. Previously, he had lived his own way and left her alone. Now he kissed her good morning and then again on his return home. He bothered to ask her what she would like to do with their evening. He wanted to discuss weekend plans, too. It was nice, but troubling, that she now had a bonafide companion in life. It only seemed to add to her confusion. She kept asking herself, *Is it too late for us as a couple?*

The kids' visit took some of the pressure off. She enjoyed them so much. Edward had a new job with which he was very happy. And as far as Melanie could tell, he was still a bachelor with friends of both genders.

Melanie, Edward, Ali, Meaghan, and Lenny went swimming. Of course Lenny didn't go in the water much, but he did sit amiably poolside, puffing on a big cigar. On another day, Lenny and Edward went golfing, their favorite sport. Melanie took Meaghan and Ali shopping and to the movies. Melanie and Meaghan talked about Meaghan's upcoming move to Florida in March and about the new baby, which was due right around that same time. Little Ali overheard this conversation, and eventually this eavesdropping necessitated a talk with the child. Grandma Melanie explained to Ali that although a little brother was coming, that she would always be Grandma's favorite little girl. That seemed to appease her. One night Lenny took them all out to dinner. It was odd for Melanie to watch the new Lenny be the perfect stepfather.

With this whirlwind of excitement, Melanie didn't get a chance to check her e-mail much. She had forgotten about it until one evening was relatively quiet at night. That night she checked her inbox and saw an e-mail from Lyle.

Greetings, Mel,

I sure do miss you—I didn't realize how the absence of you would feel. I wish we could have a latte and talk face to face again. But I am glad we are communicating frequently by e-mail. As you know, I am here for you. I'll do the best I can to be a friend and support to you. I sincerely wish I could help you get some clarity in your life. To create a soap opera was not your goal when you came to Paris, I know. I hope our friendship didn't serve to complicate your situation more. I would be horrified to have caused you any more angst. Anyway, about your husband—I certainly realize that it must be difficult for you, especially after the time in Paris with Mark. I honestly don't know what to tell you. Mark has said there is no future; at least that is how you have explained it to me. You husband offers you a future, but he may have already lost your heart. My only advice is to take your time with this one. I am here for you.

Your friend, Lyle

She typed up her return e-mail quickly.

Lyle,

You are a sweetheart. Thanks for your friendship. I will indeed take my time, but as you know, I am madly in love. By the way, how is your situation coming along? Anything turning for the better? Take care, and stay in touch.

Mel

The birthday dinner was lovely. Lenny took everyone out to Melanie's favorite restaurant. Ali was all dressed up in a new outfit they had bought her. When Lenny ordered her a Shirley Temple drink to sip along with the adults' cocktails, she was thrilled. He was thoughtful and amazed everyone. He had picked out a beautiful Cartier bracelet for Melanie; it was one that he knew she had admired, many months earlier. *He remembered!* she thought, dumbfounded. He gave it to her in front of everyone, as if to say that he was a changed man.

When the kids left, the whirlwind died down to the gentle swirl of everyday life, and she felt blessed by family. She let serenity into her heart. At work, Melanie was making progress with Stephanie, managing to show the young woman how much she had to live for and that her medical problem was solvable. She talked at length to Stephanie about living life to its fullest and letting the small stuff roll off her back. Stephanie had always been independent and healthy, and she was terrified to realize that her body was vulnerable, like everyone else's. Stephanie was beginning to "count her blessings"—being thankful for what she had, rather than dwelling on what she didn't have. She and Melanie had developed a nice acquaintance by the time she left the hospital, and Melanie was feeling pleased with her ability to comfort the young woman in her dark hours of fear.

Melanie was both satisfied and pensive on her way home that late fall afternoon. Her thoughts drifted to Mark's handsome face, as they usually did when she was in the car, alone and listening to her favorite romantic CD of Billy Joel.

At home, there was a package delivered by Federal Express at her door. It had a California return address. Once inside the front door, she tore it open. There was a gift and note that left her so weak in the knees that she had to sit down.

It was a Tiffany key on a sterling silver chain.
The note read:

Happy birthday, Mel. Here is the key to my heart.
Mark

While she was overwhelmed emotionally by the gift and the note, her heart thumped with fear. What if Lenny had come home first? Of course, while that was unlikely, she wondered what kind of scene it would have produced. She supposed that the "new and improved Lenny" could rightfully react as a jealous husband. Who knew what would happen? How he would react?

As usual she was left wondering. What did this mean? It was a new piece to the puzzle, after virtually no contact from Mark at all. She hurried to the computer.

Mark,

I received your gift. First, I love it. Your taste is impeccable, and the significance of it will be my hope. Thank you for thinking of me in this way. Second, I think you took more away from Paris than I might have realized. It is quite a surprise, as your recent silence has had me wondering.
Mel

Will he reply? she wondered anxiously. Melanie headed to the garden to collect black-eyed Susan seeds for next year. With some gusto she snipped each seed head and placed it in a paper bag. *What do I deserve in this life? What must I do to get it?* After gathering the bags, she worked to get the seeds into empty film canisters from her trip. She fretted for an hour as she worked painstakingly to save each seed, reaching the point of being drained. As she started loading the canisters into the refrigerator, she decided not to jump to conclusions. By the time she had safely tucked away the last of the seeds for spring, Melanie had achieved a state of calm.

19

Each day when she came home from work, she checked the computer, but there was no response from Mark. She wondered, with a smirk, what houses the planets were in to have left her in such a mess. So she decided to ask Lois for answers, even though she had no real belief in astrology. Besides which, she wanted to find out how Lois's river cruise plans were coming along. She remembered what Lois had warned her: Astrology was a double-edged sword. It could provide lots of answers, but one might not like all of the answers.

Melanie made a latte date with Lois at their usual coffeehouse.

"Zao shang hao," Lois greeted her.

"Zao shang hao," Melanie mimicked back. "I see you're getting in the mood."

"Yes," said Lois heartily, "and I found out that we will be having a martial arts demonstration right on the boat, and the troupe look very handsome. We're getting lessons on board, so when I get back, I will show you some of my fierce moves."

They both laughed to think of Lois, a leggy blonde, as being fierce.

"And your astrology says that you are not going to fall overboard on this trip?" Melanie joked.

"Nah, not on this trip," she smiled. "Everything should go as smooth as silk. But I have to admit, Mel, that while I really

134

believe in astrology, sometimes I'm hesitant when it comes to you."

Sipping some latte, Melanie asked, "Why?"

"Well, first, it's all so serious. Your whole life hangs in the balance. Second, I'm the one who has to give you such important information."

"Please don't worry about that. I'm a big girl, and I can take whatever life has in store for me."

"You sure?" Lois reached over and clasped her friend's hand. "I'm glad that you are finally interested in the long version of your chart. On the other hand, I'm sorry that it will be difficult to explain. As you know, I take this stuff seriously, and I have been watching your chart for the last six months now."

Lois took a moment and drew seven boxes on a napkin, labeling them one through seven. "Here's what I know," she said. "The transits are showing that Neptune is in your natal fifth house." Lois put an N in the fifth box. "Neptune represents confusion right now in the area of your life that concerns itself, among other things, with love affairs. Neptune also represents having a very idealistic view and not being in reality regarding the love affair."

"As if I'm wearing rose-colored glasses?" Melanie asked.

"Yes, that's exactly the right metaphor," Lois confirmed. "Your surprise over Lenny's behavior is due to Uranus transiting your seventh house, referring to marital partners." Lois put a U in the seventh box.

"Where Uranus is concerned," Lois said, "you need to expect the unexpected. The surprise can either be a positive event or a negative event."

"And what do you think?" Melanie asked.

Lois replied, "Well, from seeing how Uranus affects your natal chart's planets, it appears to be a welcomed surprise. I say this because transiting Uranus is 'trining' your natal Mercury, your natal Mars, and your natal Saturn."

"Okay," said Melanie. "What's a trine?"

Lois smiled. "A trine is an aspect that is auspicious, gifting you with an opportunity that you didn't even have to work for, one that just landed on your lap." Lois looked up from her latte, and her eyes locked with Melanie, who waited expectantly.

Melanie just knew that the other shoe was about to drop.

Finally Lois continued. "I do have something I feel that I need to give you a heads-up on," Lois said. She quickly added, "I'm hesitant to mention this, because it is a negative aspect."

Melanie took a breath and waited.

"Transiting Uranus is opposing your natal Neptune in your first house. When this occurs in a chart, the person may encounter strain and tension. Sometimes it signals a change of feeling or confusion."

Melanie rolled her eyes. "I can't disagree with that."

Undaunted, Lois went on. "In addition, the Uranus–Neptune opposition could possibly signify betrayal, in that it concerns the first house (yourself) and the seventh house (which is close relationships). There is potential for either of you in a close relationship to betray each other."

Melanie took it in, flat faced and then waited.

Lois sighed and finished with, "I don't want to alarm you, but as you requested the information, I needed to include all of it."

"Wow, Lois, that's complicated. Now I understand why it takes so long to do a chart. Am I to understand that either Mark or myself will be making a change, or does it have to do with Lenny or Lyle?"

"I can't say. Just know that it will be unexpected. You have come so far in the past six months. Please don't lose your hope. Mark is in your life for a purpose. He's given you a reason to get out of a corner after all these years."

"Yeah, that's for sure!" Melanie agreed.

"We share some of the same insecurities and life struggles, as you know," Lois said. "I found a man who understood me from the beginning. It didn't happen for you that way, and now you are seeing that."

Melanie nodded.

"You recently found two wonderful men, Mark and Lyle, who accept and cherish you, yet in different ways. They love all of you, as I do." Lois looked unabashedly into her friend's eyes. "You cannot be disappointed, no matter what the outcome, because in this experience, you have come out of your shell. That is important and for keeps."

Melanie let out a sigh at Lois's positive conclusion. It was something she hadn't seen before. Previously, Melanie's take on the situation was simple: You either lost at love, or you won. But what Lois pointed out had a lot of merit. In truth, Melanie hadn't yet felt a sense of losing, but rather a sense of gaining, which was an entirely new concept to her. She felt more courage, and that her life had expanded beyond the little corner where it had been. Of course, she wasn't very clear on how she felt about the more complex parts of the astrology; but all in all, it was enlightening.

"Thanks, Lois, you are a dear friend, and I appreciate your efforts and insights." She tapped on her watch, to make the point that life is fleeting. "Certainly it's a waste of time to wait around for other people to make my life exciting. Maybe I can stop trying to be what someone else wants and just be me."

When they parted, Melanie gave her friend a heartfelt and firm hug. "What would I do without you?" she murmured into her shoulder.

"Well fortunately, we are friends forever," laughed Lois.

When Melanie arrived home, she was in a pensive mood. The past six months had been a whirlwind. As Lois said, some of that whirlwind was eye opening. Melanie thought of something that she had read by Virginia Woolf, and she went online to bring up the whole quote:

"Across the broad continent of a woman's life falls the shadow of a sword. On one side, all is correct, definite, orderly. The paths are straight, the trees regular, the sun shaded: escorted by gentlemen, protected by policemen, wedded and buried by clergymen, she had only to wait demurely from cradle to grave and no one would touch a hair on her head. But on the other side, all is confusion. Nothing follows a regular course. The paths wind between bogs and precipices; the trees roar and rock and fall in ruin."

Woolf was talking about safety, of that Melanie was sure. Melanie concluded that what was happening to her was exciting, but it was also a lot more risky than remaining in her corner. The risk for her was in her allowing the inner changes she was making to become permanent, no matter what natural consequences might unfold. She also realized that her work was crucial in more than one way. Not only did it lift her from the anxiety of her love life, but it also gave her pride and a strong sense of purpose. She liked helping others and having an important role in the medical field, a profession so intense that one must be devoted entirely to a patient, since that person's life was at stake.

Later that evening, an e-mail from Mark arrived.

Hi Honey,

So glad you liked the key. You are the only one who has the key to my heart. A surprising turn of events: Susan will be on a business trip to France. Would you like to visit LA for a few days? I know you recently got back from Paris, but I thought the beginning of December would work if you can get a few days off.

She will be gone a month this time, so I'm flexible. Missing you, Mel. You are definitely impossible for me to forget.
    Mark

No doubt this would be yet another romantic encounter. But was this what she truly wanted? She really wanted permanence. She didn't want to become a jet setter. It was preferable to be a woman in love who had her man on hand every day.

It would be fun to go, but what would that solve in the end? These days, she was thinking more often about the end game. One benefit of visiting him in LA was that she would be introduced to his world. If things worked out the way she hoped, that world would also become hers. She wanted to see him in his routine life. Maybe some of his romantic allure would fade.

When they were with each other, they didn't talk about life's everyday problems. They were like two teenagers in love. So far their time together had been memorable, but they were avoiding any important decisions. They were not making progress to a more permanent, happy life.

Should she go? It was almost a superfluous question. How could she resist? The man was so damn romantic, and she was too curious about how he'd look on his own turf. *Am I hooked on love?* She thought about that for a moment. *I can think of worse things to be addicted to.*

20

As the aircraft lifted off, Melanie felt the little lurch in her stomach, and then she settled back to think. This was becoming all too familiar: giving Lenny a story about why she was going someplace, sitting in an aircraft, thinking about Mark and anticipating being with him once more. *If we were married, could the excitement be maintained?* She decided that it wasn't reasonable to expect passion like this to last. She reasoned, *No old married couples feel this kind of anticipation and excitement—this titillating, almost perverse excitement.*

Perhaps this time, Mark would make a commitment. Much to her embarrassment, she even said out loud on the plane, *Will we always be clandestine lovers? Or will we get married?* People around her stared, and she shrugged back.

It had been six months since their first meeting. Her life was richer in so many ways. *Why am I still doing this? Should this be the last time? Am I strong enough to let him go?* As for Mark's family problems, she was beginning to doubt the truth of this story. Moreover, Mark had started to seem different to her. She couldn't put her finger on it. Was it the reliance on e-mail, over phone calls? Or was it the tone of the e-mails? It was too subtle to figure out, but there was definitely something up. *Is he hiding something? Is he telling me the truth? Is he as much in love with me as he said? If he is, why wouldn't he be making plans for us to be together?* After all, they had talked about being together since their first encounter.

As the flight droned on, Melanie continued to think. Marriage and life-long commitment were what she truly wanted. When the plane was nearing its destination and the pilot announced that they would be landing at LAX in twenty minutes, she went over her hair and makeup. *Is everything just right?* Sitting in a plane for three and a half hours could mess up anybody's appearance. She dabbed some perfume behind her ears, checked her makeup in her hand mirror, and fussed with her hair. Walking to baggage claim with the usual jitters, she realized how well acquainted she was with these feelings about him. Then there was the familiar lurch of her heart when she spotted him.

There he was, waiting at the baggage carousel, dressed in a black polo shirt and tan slacks. He was wearing expensive Italian loafers with no socks. She threw herself into his arms, smiling. "My, how California we look," she said approvingly.

He grinned. "And how pretty you are, as usual." Holding her back a bit, Mark gazed at her. "You blow me away, honey. I missed you so." They grabbed her suitcases and headed for the car. She was surprisingly calm. Was it just being with him that mellowed her out? His presence somehow always made her feel safe.

He checked them into a boutique hotel in the Hollywood Hills. It was a spa and most discreet. "Unwind and pamper yourself," he directed. "I'll be back for dinner, and then I promise I'm all yours." That wasn't a surprise, as he was always busy. What was a surprise was the room itself. Rose petals covered the floor, and in a trail led up to a four-poster bed that was so plush and heavy it looked like a prop in a period movie. A white, see-through baby doll nightie lay on the bed. Chocolate kisses from a luxury specialty shop tastefully graced the night table. The stage was certainly set for romance. Melanie thought, *Is this over the top, or what? Maybe it's a goodbye date.*

She unpacked, got comfortable, and went out on the terrace. Nearby palm trees swayed, and to Melanie it looked like their fronds were caressing one another in a most serene way. The chirping of the phone drew her back; it was a text message from Mark. "Honey, I hope you visit the spa. There is something special waiting there for a special woman." *Would this ever stop? Was this the kiss off?*

She went down to the spa, still in the blue-ruffled dress that he liked. They were expecting her. Set out for her were a glass of her favorite Riesling, chilled to perfection, a soft terrycloth robe, and flip flops. A young Chinese woman with a subtle smile ushered her into the massage room. She had never been in such a room: soft lights and perfumed candles cast erotic shadows on the walls. Two massage beds, side by side, awaited. Mark lay in one. She again was awed by his attention to detail. She was whisked away to a sensuous world. Wonderful, talented hands massaged their naked bodies. Though they shared the room with the two masseuse, Mark and Melanie bonded at a new level, as if their bodies had co-joined.

Back in the room, feeling loose and relaxed, Mark gazed at Melanie and murmured, "I want you, honey." He removed each item of her clothing slowly and thoughtfully. First was her short ruffled dress, then her lingerie. He commented on her black lace thong, even as he unhooked her bra.

Now naked, she no longer felt self-conscious, but at ease. He pulled her close and began trailing kisses over her torso. He seemed more deliberate than ever before, as though he was worshipping her body and didn't want to miss anything. He talked to her, telling her what he was going to do before he did it.

While his attitude was worshipful, hers was focused on giving. She no longer worried about it ending. She was fully in the moment and lost in his kisses and caresses. She was awash in emotion, shivering with desire. She kept thinking, *I would do anything for you.* At this moment, Melanie was truly his slave. Strong physical feelings consumed her. Finally came the explosion and the blessed, liberating release.

As she lay beside him, for a scant moment she wondered if it was time for answers and stability. Then an unusual thing happened. Before she could catch her breath, he was awakening her senses again. His lips on her belly leading up to her breasts were so distracting and surprising, that she found herself panting with renewed desire. Then he was plunging into the depths of her, and with him she achieved a heartfelt release. They both slipped into a deep sleep.

When she awoke, a new question haunted her. Was this reality, or was her life back home reality?

Over the next few days, she became acquainted with quite a bit of Mark's world. With his wife thousands of miles away on business, they spent the night in a guest room in his home. She was stunned by the sheer extravagance of the estate. They played tennis at the estate's court. They had drinks on the patio. He had dinner catered and served to them. As they watched the sunset, he asked, "Are you a good sailor?"

"I don't know. Why? Or should I guess?"

"That's right. In the morning, we're going sailing."

The next day was spectacular weather, and the Pacific was sparkling and blue. They left the yacht club after breakfast and set a course for Catalina Island, about twenty miles out. He stood behind her and guided her as she steered the boat to his directions. She relished the wind in their faces. She didn't even worry about her hair getting windblown. She kept a steady grip on the wheel while he went below. He returned in a while with a platter of food he'd bought at a deli: roast beef and Swiss on fresh French bread, olives, pickles, potato salad, and white Reisling wine. They munched happily as the low-lying island came into view. In another half hour, they had set the anchor in the harbor at Avalon, the island's main town. They finished the wine as they gazed at the red-tiled roofs of the island's dwellings. Off to the right on a point, a large building dominated the view.

"What's that?" she asked.

"A casino, one of the first in California. And see that mansion way up there at the peak of that hill? That's the Wrigley mansion. You know, Wrigley's gum?"

When they finished the wine, they went ashore and rented a small surry-topped jeep. They'd seen an army of them scooting around the island. It was fun. At the top of one hill, they came upon a herd of buffalo. Mark was driving. He stopped. One buffalo's big shaggy head loomed above the jeep's windshield. Melanie screeched. The beast kept chomping grass and staring at them. Mark grinned. "Don't worry, they're harmless. They were left here years ago by a movie company filming on the island."

For Melanie's peace of mind, he quickly left the area. But Catalina kept giving up great secrets. From some high points, the vistas of the sweeping Pacific were panoramic and magnificent.

After exploring the island, with Mark as their excellent guide, they set sail and arrived back at the yacht club in the late afternoon. They spent cocktail time aboard with a pitcher of Margaritas. By nightfall, they were back at his house. With all the activity and late-night lovemaking, Melanie was exhausted. Just before she drifted off, he said, "Get some sleep. Tomorrow's going to be a big day."

Her eyes widened. "And?"

"We're going to drive up the coast to Big Sur. You know, Monterey."

The next day on the drive up the coast, there were quiet times. Melanie thought, *How can I ever go back? This is fabulous. I know Lenny wants me, but that's not enough to win back my heart after years of ignoring me.*

But what about Mark? Surely he isn't giving up his wife and life here in California.

She'd seen photos around the house of Mark and his family boating, skiing, and having birthday parties. Naturally these pictures were only snapshots out of time and didn't necessarily reflect his life now; but still she could sense why he was reluctant to leave. In fact, there was no indication that he was ever going to leave. She made a mental note not to attend the reunion. No use in seeing him if she couldn't have him, she reasoned.

I have to have a plan, she thought. *I have to find happiness without him.*

Around midday and about two hundred and fifty miles north of Los Angeles, Mark slowed the big Mercedes and pulled off the highway. Melanie saw the signs for Hearst Castle. Mark said, "You're gonna love this place. Randolph Hearst's family gave it to the state of California some years ago."

It looked like a huge Spanish church, with twin spires between its white adobe center. It was nestled between the Santa Lucia Mountains and the Pacific at about sixteen hundred feet up. They spent a fascinating afternoon touring the castle and grounds. Later, at dinnertime, Mark found a charming bed and breakfast just off the main highway to San Francisco. For once since she'd been in California, charm was trumping luxury. She adored the place, with its cozy rooms, home-cooked meals, and the ocean vistas. It wasn't ostentatious in any way, and somehow it fit Melanie's mood. She was worried that the ultra-luxury she had been experiencing would jade her and distort her thinking. Even without what luxuries Mark's money could buy, she'd still take him if he could be hers alone.

In the morning they continued north. Around lunchtime they arrived on the Monterey Peninsula, that place of ocean vista and unique fauna. "Look," Mark pointed out. "There's the famous lone eucalyptus tree you see on all the calendars. Isn't it cool?"

Melanie didn't say anything, but she was studying the tree.

"What?" he asked, curious about her mesmerized gazing. "In the end, it's only a tree."

"Why is it that I feel somehow in tune with that tree?"

"Why would you? It's wind swept, twisted, and old. Nothing like you."

"I don't mean I look like it, silly! But there's something about its lonely place in the world. Alone, overlooking an amazing seascape."

Mark missed her meaning. He continued the popular seventeen-mile drive, showing her the sights as they headed up the coast toward San Jose and then San Francisco.

The "City on the Bay" was fun. They rode the cable cars, ate at a great Chinese restaurant in Chinatown, and had cocktails on the terrace of the St. Marks Hotel, high atop Russian Hill, offering one of the most amazing views in America.

Eventually her stay was at an end. At the airport, they kissed goodbye, but she didn't tell him it was their last kiss. Deeply in love, the tears welling in her eyes, she walked down the aisle of the plane to find her seat back to reality. Her joy at having been with him turned to pain. There would be no other trips. She was determined.

21

Melanie was on the cusp of a new life. True, it wasn't the fantasy that she had dreamed of, which of course was a life with Mark. But Mark had been the catalyst. In reaching out to her, he had shown her that she was still desirable and that she did not have to get dusty, stored away on a shelf. She wasn't old, and she didn't have to settle. He had shaken her up and dismantled many of her fears and self-doubts. She would never forget him.

The trip to California had been the turning point. As soon as she saw him in his world, it was clear that she was not going to be a part of it. The visit had been the ultimate fantasy of what life could be like and an everlasting memory. She knew that the heart was truly a lonely hunter, and even though her heart had found love, it apparently was simply not to be. Her only choice was to learn from the experience.

Now came the most difficult part: breaking up. She realized that she could only have a new beginning if she had an ending. As she wrote the letter, she cried.

Dear Mark,

I don't know how I can even write this, but I know I must. I have fallen deeply in love with you. You have shown me what true acceptance is, and for that I am grateful. You have helped me to unleash my inner desires, and you allowed me to experience my dreams in a way I never thought possible. You have given me youth, zest for life on my terms, and forgiveness for all my transgressions. You have shown me that I am much more than a pretty face—that I am a good person.

These are gifts I will treasure on my journey.

I had wished my life journey would be with you. But now I realize how impossible that is for you. I respect what you need to do, and now you must respect me. I never would have pursued a relationship with you if I hadn't believed in my heart that you were going to be free. Breaking up a family was never my intention. I know that you thought you were going to be free also; but I think as you imagined the damage and destruction it might cause all the people around you, you couldn't bring yourself to leave them.

You're thinking first of others, which is one of the reasons I love you. So you see how I understand you, honey.

With an aching heart, I must say goodbye, at least for now. I do not regret our time together. I will never forget a moment of it.

Know that every day I will send you love and light as I think about you. You will be in my heart as I wear your key.

I will keep our memories close.

If anything changes for you, please let me know.

Until some other time, I remain,

Your high school Goddess,

Melanie

She read back the e-mail to make sure she could send it. She hoped he would understand that he controlled their fate. Ending things was not usually her forté, but the letter did sound final enough.

As she pushed the send key, the tears kept rolling down her cheeks.

22

There were days that she very much regretted sending the e-mail, but in the back of her mind, she knew it was the right thing to do. Melanie fantasized daily about what response she wanted from him, which was for him to offer to marry her and divorce Susan.

There was a lot for Melanie to prepare for. Meaghan would soon be arriving in Florida, and there would be a new baby to take care of. Melanie spent her days working at the hospital and looking forward to Meaghan's arrival. Lois would be back from China soon with lots of stories and photos. Melanie started to think that maybe in the next few years, she would retire.

Reunion e-mail news was coming again as the date grew closer. People were attending mini-reunions, and in fact there was one coming up in Boca. She could probably convince Lois to go with her.

One afternoon on the way home from work, she had an inkling. Sure enough, when she logged in, there it was: an e-mail from Mark. At first she was afraid to open it. What if he agreed with her, and it really was over? If they were not moving toward marriage, she knew it was the only way to move on.

Melanie,

Wow, I didn't expect that e-mail. After getting over my shock and disappointment, I can finally respond. I do agree with your decision. Regrettably so; but intellectually, I get it. After you left California, I had been thinking along the same lines, but couldn't bring myself to say the final goodbye. Our time together was so perfect, I couldn't bear to think it would be our last. After all these years of wanting you, my dream came true, so it was hard to accept an end to the dream. I hope you know how much I care for you and love you, often beyond my ability to find the words to convey the emotions to you. Our circumstances script our future, and right now we are not at the same place. What I do know is this: I am certain that you will find a great love in your life someday. After all, such a beautiful person as you will undoubtedly meet up with someone who will be able to cherish all of you without limitations.

So Mel, it seems as if we have come to the end of this journey. I have enjoyed every minute of it and will miss you daily. I will go to bed thinking of you and will wake up with a picture of you in my mind and thoughts of you in my heart. Thank you for accepting the key to my heart. My heart is eternally yours, and only yours.
Mark

She stared at the words, crying. Her dream was shattered. He had accepted the end relatively easily, so that he didn't have to inconvenience Susan, face his children, and give up part of his lifestyle. That being so, Melanie knew she had been the adult. She had chosen the right path if he was not ready for commitment; but right now, it felt so wrong. She knew she was making space for the new opportunities yet to be known. But how would she endure the pain? The courage she had developed this year showed her that she could do hard things. She remembered a passage from *The Road Less Traveled,* by M. Scott Peck: "Once we truly know that life is difficult—once we truly understand and accept it—then life is no longer difficult. Because once it is accepted, the fact that life is difficult no longer matters."

23

Melanie's challenges at work allowed time to pass fairly quickly. But she wasn't "back to normal," because Mark had changed her life. Melanie would never be the same. She had learned, albeit the hard way, that she was still a hot babe. She no longer felt outdated, desired only by Schneider. Melanie did everything she could to keep busy when home from work. She even went to one of the mini re-unions alone, as Lois would have nothing to do with it.

Her relationship with Lenny was at an odd place. While they both tried hard to reconnect, she could not find fulfillment with him. No amount of romantic dinners made a difference. It was of little consequence that now he was a super-attentive lover. He had let her languish too long, and he had lost her heart.

She remembered her mother telling her that she had to do everything possible to keep a man—so why was she considering divorcing Lenny? Because she had learned self-sufficiency. If no one else was around to offer comfort, she could bolster herself. In the last year, she had found that out, and more. With time, the pain would dissipate; how could she ever look back on this year as anything but wonderful?

She was pleased to discover that Lyle wanted to visit New York with her. Meeting him there would pose no problem, because Lenny knew about him, and there was no jealousy about Melanie's friendship with Lyle.

A few days later, on the way home from work, she got a phone call from Lyle. Indeed, he had decided to come to New York and said that he would love to see her. In fact, he was calling her from New York. They discussed plans to meet. This trip would afford Melanie an opportunity to make a quick visit to Meaghan's. She could help her with the packing.

She met Lyle at the Russian Tea Room, one of his favorite spots in New York. He looked even more wonderful than she remembered. She noticed that he was dressed a bit less formally than when they were in Europe. Of course, "casual" for Lyle meant that he was wearing a sweater vest rather than his customary tweed jacket and bowtie.

After they got caught up, she saw Lyle gazing at the vivid red and green room with its samovars. The samovars (ornate Russian vessels used to boil water) were as ornate as the rest of the place.

Lyle smiled. Melanie asked, "What has tickled your funny bone?"

Lyle grinned. "They say the English have a love for extravagance. Yet look at those samovars! In England, they would simply use a tea kettle; but the Russians have elevated boiling water to an art form."

Melanie said, "I've never been here. It's so …"

"Excessive?" he asked, smiling.

"Yes. I guess that's it. Everything is so super gaudy and ornate."

Lyle said, "But it hasn't always been so. Back in the twenties, the poor Polish and Russian immigrants came here to have tea, jam, and cookies."

Melanie asked, "Was that a specialty back then?"

"No, it was all they could afford."

After lunch, they toured Manhattan. He knew so much about New York, and Lyle shared Melanie's enthusiasm for all the city had to offer. He pointed out the eclectic architecture, which covered every decade since the nineteenth century. As usual, Lyle the historian was fascinating.

They sat in Battery Park at the tip of Manhattan, gazing into the wide Hudson River. They were quietly sipping tea when a thoughtful Melanie said, "Have you ever wondered about the haphazard nature of our lives?"

He turned to her. "You mean our lives—you and I?"

"No. I mean all people. You meet people throughout your life; but the question is, do you meet them in the right order? What of the person you want to spend the rest of your life with? What if you don't meet your dream mate early enough in life?"

Lyle, too, lapsed thoughtful. "Or never at all," he mused.

There was something very personal and profound in that comment. She didn't question him further, not wanting to perhaps open up some old wound. But she couldn't help thinking about her high school days, when she was so caught up in being sought after by the older guys. Had she really been so blinded to what really mattered?

Lyle eventually revealed to Melanie that he had a new Parisian love, closer to his own age. He found that they had so much more in common. Lyle seemed happy about it, although mysteriously wistful. When they talked about Mark, Lyle simply offered his everlasting support of any decision that she made.

After a three-day visit, which both enjoyed thoroughly, Lyle saw her off at Grand Central Station. She was taking the Amtrak to Boston to visit Meaghan. He walked her right down to the train steps and then kissed her with what she sensed as a bit more affection than usual. She was pleased. She thanked him for a wonderful time, and they both promised to write as soon as they got home.

Meaghan was thrilled to see her mother just when she needed help. They had fun packing and chatting. Melanie found little Ali more engaging since she saw her last. She commented, "She's just like you, Meaghan—chatty and charming!"

Melanie asked her pregnant daughter how she was feeling and inquired if they had decided on a name for the baby yet. Meaghan said it was going to be a surprise and wouldn't spill the beans.

Then she told her daughter, "If your experience in moving to Florida is anything like mine, the state is going to take some getting used to. But Delray Beach has a nice climate. Although summers are hot, you have the cooling breezes off the ocean. I think you're going to like it."

After a delightful visit with Meaghan, on the flight home Melanie thought, *There is so much to tell Lois about! Good thing she's on her way home and did not decide to buy a houseboat on the Yangtze. I wonder what the planets are up to? If I ever was curious to know, it's now.*

24

Sitting by the pool at Lois's house was so much fun. The friends were deep into their conversation. Lois, impervious to the hot noonday sunshine, was wearing her prize acquisition from China: a conical bamboo hat. Lois excitedly related how dolphins came right up to their boat. She showed off the Shaolin scorpion kick, which did indeed, make her look fierce. Melanie, for her part, covered Lyle's assessment of the architecture of Manhattan. It had been several months since Melanie had last heard from Mark, so she really didn't have anything new to relate from him. She put her drink down and lamented, "I know I ended it, but somehow I didn't think he would let it stick."

She'd said it with a far-off stare. "There hasn't been a day I haven't missed him or thought of him. Lenny's been asking me why I wear this key. He doesn't seem to believe my story about where it came from." She sat back in her lounge chair and sighed. "I hate being deceitful. Maybe I should confess to Lenny about the whole thing. I'm sure he would divorce me if he knew."

Lois said, "Go slowly. You've emerged from your shell, and I don't want you to lose that, ever again."

Melanie didn't seem to be taking solace in her friend's words, even though she was listening intently.

Lois continued, "We change in life. If we don't change, we are not growing. You are changing. Remember when I told you about the planet Uranus? The planet Uranus is all about change. It is an awakening. For you, this change is regarding your partner and close relationships. You are no longer who you once were—Nevertheless, you are not yet who you are about to become. Your personality is in a transformative state."

"I believe you are right. I saw a butterfly in Paris and thought the same thing. It's like I'm emerging from a cocoon, out of an existence that was safe and predictable to a world where anything can happen." She threw her arms out to encompass the sky. "Isn't it scary? Our lives are so fleeting. You know an adult butterfly probably has an average life span of approximately one month. Life is so short, that I want to make it count and not put things off for a future time."

Melanie smiled and tapped Lois on the hand. "Remember when we used to play hopscotch on the driveway?"

"Yeah," Lois chuckled. "I'd always ask you if I could have a 'do over' because I didn't like my throws."

"Exactly," Melanie said, snapping her fingers. "I always said yes. But in real life, there is no one to ask for a do over. What we do each day is stamped in our history. If I could, I would go back to high school and talk to that kid in the last row and ask him for a date, even if we had to walk because he didn't yet have his license. I play that scene over in my mind. It haunts me."

Lois leaned forward, her eyes full of compassion. "You have become the 'role model' of the youngest sixty-six-year-old woman I know. Don't drag yourself back to dwell in the past when you have a wide-open future in front of you."

Melanie absently twirled a strand of hair. "Part of moving forward is leaving Lenny. He ignored me for so long, that I don't feel adoring of him anymore. Fear of being alone has kept me in a relationship prison for too long, but I don't fear much these days. Does my plan sound too risky?"

Not missing a beat, Lois said, "No, you sound like a woman who is looking at her life and her options very carefully and realistically."

With a wistful smile, Melanie said, "It's funny how different our lives have been. You married the man you will be with forever, and I married twice yet have still not found that."

Lois nodded in empathy. "Yes, but look at what you did get—the daughter I always wanted. How could I have had two boys? I do love them, but there was never a chance to buy frilly little dresses. Just years of sneakers, jeans, and t-shirts!"

Melanie laughed. "Those boys ran you ragged, didn't they? Like little monkeys, climbing on everything. They were so cute."

"Yep, they were. Always in trouble, too!" Lois grinned.

Melanie turned serious. "You know, when I close my eyes every night, I find myself with Mark. So I know I can do anything, because he gave me the key not only to his heart but also to life as it is yet to unfold. All I have to do is try to open the door."

Putting her hand on her friend's shoulder supportively, Lois said, "I know how you struggle with this one. No one can tell you which path to take. We need to live in the moment, but that task, of course, is easier said than done. I know you don't want to go through another divorce, but only you can decide to take yet another risk. Let me tell you where you are, as your chart has been pretty accurate so far."

Melanie appreciated her friend's concern and said, "Sure Lois, I'm up for it. What do you see happening in the next few months that I should be aware of?"

There was that always-noticeable (though almost imperceptible) change in Lois's voice when she started getting into a reading. She normally rattled off the houses and planets with authority and panache. With the bamboo hat on, today she sounded like a Chinese scholar. She said, "Pluto is sextiling your natal Jupiter in your second house. This action signifies a rebirth of your self-esteem, the gift you say is from Mark. It is also seen in all the support of your good friend, Lyle. He has been instrumental in showing you your value and how much he respects you for all you are. (In much the same way I see you, too, I must say.) I am so glad he entered your life. Transiting Jupiter in your ninth house is 'gifting' Neptune. Now you should be able to make logical decisions about relationships, and the answer will come to you."

"It does make sense," Melanie said, "and I do feel that I am changing in a lot of ways. For one thing," she explained, "I am not sure that I can continue this marriage with the feelings I have. I have a different perspective on the relationship I want and need. I have experienced a relationship on deeper levels, and I want it. I also know it can be had in the real world, not just in fantasy, and I have Mark to thank for that. I may need to tell him so one day."

Seemingly pleased by such a well-articulated response, Lois simply asked, "And so?"

"So my next move is to talk to Lenny. He did change for the better, and he doesn't deserve someone next to him just going through the motions."

"You're a good woman," Lois said, standing up. "I hope that Lenny can appreciate it. Before you leave, let me show you what I made for you in calligraphy class on the boat." She ducked into the house and returned with a rolled, rice parchment, secured shut with a red ribbon. Melanie undid the ribbon and pulled the scroll open. In the middle was the Chinese symbol for heart, which Lois had made carefully with brush and ink: 心

And under that, in English, Lois had written this old Chinese proverb:

Wherever you go, go with all your heart. If you always give, you will always have.

25

The upcoming talk with Lenny had been gnawing away at Melanie, and she wanted the talk to be over. But life got in the way, and discussing the divorce with Lenny got postponed.

Her daughter's family flew down for the move to Florida, because the drive would have been very uncomfortable for Meaghan at nine months pregnant. Problems developed with the long-distance move; the van with their furniture had been diverted at Virginia Beach for a Navy shipment. Melanie had to stay in touch with the van line to find out where the furniture was and when it would arrive. Concurrently, Meaghan was about to deliver the baby. Because the furniture wasn't on schedule, Melanie had to ask a neighbor to be at the new house to accept the furniture delivery. Jim and Meaghan were at the hospital, checking out the contractions that she started having once they arrived in Florida. Melanie, meanwhile, was busy at home, keeping close tabs on Ali.

Spending time with her four-year-old grandchild always took Melanie's breath away. True, the precocious child was a handful, and it had been a long time since Melanie had to keep up with an active little one. The child remembered everything she was ever told, taught, or read. Ali could out run and out talk her grandmother and always remained one step ahead of Melanie's logic. But it was well worth it. Ali amazed and amused everyone, most of all Melanie. She decided to take Ali to the mall for lunch and then to the carousel and bookstore.

Melanie was glad she could be of help to Meaghan and Jim by having Ali stay for a while. For so long, because they lived out of state, she couldn't do the mother-in-law and grandmother things she wanted so desperately to do. Now was her chance, so she offered to keep Ali for as long as needed, even if she had to call out of work.

Melanie and Ali had a blast at the mall. The bookstore was the highlight of the day. Ali, who was already able to read, picked out three books and a baby book for her new brother who would be arriving any day. That she was such a thoughtful child, just made you love her more. Lenny offered to take them out to dinner at any place Ali chose. She was not too picky about location, but restaurants with coloring activities took priority.

In the evening, after getting Ali to sleep, Melanie was dog tired but content. Before drifting off, she contemplated how much her life had changed in the last nine months. Her life was certainly on an upswing. She knew that to find the adventure and romance that she sought in life, she was going to have to go out and make it happen.

She wondered how Mark was. She had finally become used to not hearing from him, although she missed him terribly. Lois and Lyle were very special to her, and she was glad to have their support as she attempted to move on. Many times she struggled with an impulse to send Mark an e-mail or to call him. She had offset those urges with another activity. She lived vicariously in the memories they shared, and sometimes those memories still felt real. As she thought of Paris, she fell into a deep sleep.

Early the next morning, Melanie answered the phone and it was Jim saying that Meaghan was about to deliver. Melanie was excited and told Lenny. When Ali awoke, Melanie told her the news, too: her new brother was on the way. The three of them had pancakes and discussed it. Ali promised that she would be a great big sister. She also surreptitiously slipped Schneider an entire pancake.

Hours later, the next call arrived from Jim. The baby boy had arrived, and Meaghan was fine. The newborn was eight pounds, twenty inches long, had light-colored hair, and a perfect Apgar score of ten.

The three of them got ready to visit the hospital. Getting dressed, Ali was asking all sorts of questions. She proceeded to grill her Melanie about Apgar scores. Melanie explained the criteria for a positive Apgar score. Ali then wanted to know what hers had been at birth. Melanie wondered if the new grandson would eventually be as inquisitive.

Arriving at the hospital, they got clearance to go to the third floor. Meaghan looked great, and Jim was holding the baby when they entered the room. He immediately bent down and showed Ali her new brother, saying, "Meet Mark Joshua."

"Hello there," Ali said, on her best behavior.

Jim had also gotten Ali a t-shirt that said, "I am a Big Sister," which she promptly donned over her other clothes.

Melanie almost lost her footing when she heard that name! It was obvious to everyone, especially Lenny, that she was startled, which Melanie explained as due to not having eaten enough during the excitement.

Jim handed the baby to Melanie. Holding her grandson sent all kinds of emotions through her. He was so sweet and filled her with joy. But she knew that for the rest of her days, the name Mark would be in her life.

Now what? Melanie had to process this new part of her puzzle. Was this child's name meant to be? Was this twist a part of her chart that had been hidden by an eclipse?

26

Eventually Ali went back home, giving Melanie time to discuss with Lenny the idea of a divorce. When she looked at the bathroom mirror, the image staring back at her was a modern woman, well dressed in the latest fashion, with a young hair style and super-trim body. She knew that she could make it on her own, and that it was never too late for romance to be around the corner. While her outward appearance gave her poise, her inner strength provided confidence. Further, she knew that she had supportive friends and family, not to mention Schneider.

Melanie was determined to be loved unconditionally. It was true that she had a few quirks that she'd expect someone to live with, such as needing to talk as a couple rather that count on smoke signals or telepathy. Previously, she'd suppress things about herself, such as talking about her emotions, in order to be accepted. She had even stooped sometimes to letting a man win at Scrabble.

She decided that from now on, she would take responsibility for herself. This was not anyone else's job. Previously, in desperation, she had tried to push a man to be her savior, demanding that her needs be met, and then feeling disappointed by her partner when it didn't happen the way she had planned.

In the past, all her encounters with men usually ended up with her trying to sublimate things about herself to be accepted. Her romantic record wasn't stellar, but from now on she would not be sublimating, but rather bringing a whole person (with everything she was made of) to any relationship she entered into. She was ready to be in the last and most significant relationship of her life.

She hoped not to hurt Lenny. He had changed so much, and he didn't deserve to feel bad about this. While she was somewhat nervous, the time was right. Lenny had just come home from a golf game, and he was in a good mood.

Melanie was beginning to feel that she was becoming a pro at breakups since the infamous e-mail to Mark a few months ago. It wasn't an endearing trait in her favor. She had to jump in and do it.

He slung his golf clubs in the front hall closet.

"How was your afternoon?" Melanie greeted him.

"I was really on my game today. Wanna go grab a burger with me up at the Grill?"

"Good idea," she replied. "I have lots to talk about."

They went to the local pub. The place wasn't as busy as usual, and she picked an out-of-the-way corner table. They sat down and ordered. He got a beer, and Melanie asked for a glass of white wine. As Melanie was gathering her strength, Lenny was catching peeks at the sports TV mounted high up over the bar.

She sipped some wine and made eye contact with him. He drew his eyes from the TV screen. She said, "You realize that we have not been very connected lately. We seem to have been going our separate ways and off doing different things."

At this point he interjected, "What do you mean? I thought things were going better for a change."

"I know. You've stepped up to the plate and have done some very nice things for me and the kids. I do appreciate that. But it goes a lot deeper."

Lenny peered at her intently, which she was not accustomed to. "Mel, this is sounding ominous. Are you preparing me for something?"

"In thinking about our years together, there have been some wonderful memories. But lately I feel we are not good together anymore. I don't feel fulfilled, and I don't think you are, either."

He swigged his beer and lowered his eyes. "Actually, I was thinking along the same lines lately, but I didn't want to bring it up. I thought it would work itself out, as we men generally think. But I was wondering if something else was going on, like if there is someone else. You certainly have been paying a lot more attention to your appearance, and while you do look amazing, it has kept me wondering."

Caught by surprise, Melanie decided that because he had asked, she would tell him the truth. "Yes, there was someone else. It didn't last very long."

Lenny swallowed hard.

She gently put her hand over his hand. "I'm sorry. I know it's a shock."

"Where did this happen?" he demanded, sounding bitter, pulling his hand away. "Did you bring him to our home?"

"No, not at our home."

"Then where?" Now his eyes dilated. "Wait. All those trips? Paris and all?"

She dropped her head. "Yes."

Their booth became a silent oasis in the buzz of the restaurant.

Melanie finally said, "I am so sorry for hurting you. It is something that plagues me daily. I did fall in love with him, but I ended it."

Lenny's demeanor told her he was deep in thought. Pain wreathed his face. His voice weak, he asked, "Do you still see him now?"

"No. There's been no contact, but I think of him frequently."

His watery eyes searched hers. "But why? What caused this? Did I do something to push you into it?"

Averting his eyes, she replied, "I don't think so. You and I did separate things for so many years, and I stopped relating to you. You were in your own world, and I was in mine. I felt my life was on auto pilot; I was living day to day, but without experiencing anything new. Lately you've been great, but I can't get back my old feelings. The affair pried me loose from my hum-drum existence. I feel changed, and I'm ready to do something different."

He dropped his face into his hands. When he raised his head, he said, "I didn't expect this. I was so busy with my own life, that I didn't see yours. I can't fault you for this, even though I am saddened by the outcome. So now what do we do?"

"I really don't like divorce, but that's what I am proposing. You're a good man. I know you could be happier with someone who shares your interests, such as a lady who golfs. I'm sure you found me to be a 'high-maintenance' type of woman, because I'm so emotional, and I need to talk about it. I tried to tone down my feelings, which was okay for a while, but I can't do it any longer—it just isn't me."

Lenny seemed to be transitioning from his initial shock and anger, and he now appeared to be acknowledging that what was happening between them was inevitable.

"We both have a lot of good years left, Lord willing, don't you think?" Melanie asked.

Lenny nodded yes and said simply, "I will miss you."

A tear went down her cheek, and she reached for his hand, saying, "As I have gotten older, time has taken on another meaning. I feel that I need to do something else."

"But don't you think there is anything we can do to avoid this ending?" he pleaded. "I could try. I do love you."

"I love you, too; but I've changed, and my heart is not the same. I have thought about us in many ways, and staying together is not what I want any more. I am sorry."

Though still melancholy, Lenny seemed a bit brighter. "What you say is so on target. I know what you mean about seeing time differently now than when we were younger. Too bad time is not like my car, which I can just shift into reverse. I want to remain friends. I don't regret any of the time we've had together."

"I very much appreciate your understanding, and yes, I want to remain friends. Because Meaghan and Jim just had the baby, I'd like to wait a while before we tell them. Do you think you can do that?"

"Of course. Who knows? Maybe during that time, we can find each other again."

"As we don't have a lot of legalities to sort out, we can afford to wait a few weeks. But I don't want to feel pressured to change my mind."

"Yes, you're right, of course," he said. "Does this mean that while we are still together, you aren't going to let me win Scrabble?"

They finished their dinner on an upbeat note, and then went home to watch television. Melanie was wondering if she should e-mail Mark to say she was free, but she decided against it. She did decide, however, to go to the reunion. Lois was still adamant against it, but Melanie had to see Mark again. The list of graduates showed he was coming, and that he was coming alone.

Later that evening she dashed off an e-mail to Lyle, telling him that she had finally broached the topic of divorce with Lenny. She wondered how he would respond, as he probably never expected her to be this bold. She valued their friendship and wished he lived closer. But in some ways, e-mails were better, because he answered so quickly.

Drifting off to sleep that night, she was again pensive. She'd just ended her second marriage. Had she done the right thing? Decisions never had been her strong suit.

27

Mark wondered how Melanie was. Every day he woke up with her on his mind, and he couldn't shake it. It had been four months since he'd had any contact with her, and he missed her, finding himself doing a double take at any woman who looked like her from a distance. *How foolish of me,* he thought. *What are the chances she'd be here?*

His life was busy with work, golfing, and boating. But his mind was never free of her: the way she held her fork, the way she tossed her hair. He even admired the way she giggled at something inappropriate, getting him to giggle with her. Most of all, he liked having someone to talk to. Melanie talked often about her emotions, so he knew what she was feeling. In contrast, Susan had always been so practical and rarely spoke about how she felt. How was he supposed to know what Susan was feeling? *Perhaps Susan wants me to be telepathic,* he thought bitterly.

Whenever he thought of calling Melanie, he stopped short, not wanting to hurt her. But the inclination to talk to her kept growing stronger.

He'd need help to get over her, he decided. Cold turkey wasn't working. Even his double-booked work calendar didn't help. He spent his time at the big estate alone, because Susan was away more than she was home.

Mark wasn't especially keen on the idea of the class reunion. Yet he couldn't get it out of his head that she might be there. Could they work out these problems between them? Could he make the break and get a divorce? Did Melanie still want him? Was she willing to leave her husband? He realized that if he was honest about it, he should divorce Susan anyway; she ignored him, and he did not love her anymore. His children should be old enough by now to understand such things.

Whenever he asked himself if he could live without Melanie, she came roaring back into his mind, as if to remind him of the impossibility of being without her.

Susan had been in northern France for quite a while on this trip. That many of her clients lived there seemed to suit her. In the morning, she'd be returning.

Mark got up the gumption to be honest with her and ask for a divorce. The kids were all grown, and his oldest son's finances had gotten back on track. There was no excuse other than inertia, or cowardice. Or both.

For all he knew, Melanie might have lost respect for him, due to his vacillation. He could see that Melanie had admired his lifestyle, but she might ultimately have considered him a coward. Whether Melanie was still available or not, he knew that divorcing Susan was the right thing to do. It was becoming more hurtful to him to stay in the sterile marriage than leave.

As for his lifestyle, he would give it all up to have Melanie back in his life. It was a cliché that all the toys in the world couldn't make you happy. But he knew firsthand that his luxuries were of little comfort when he felt his heart was breaking. Without Melanie, he was overcome by a great emptiness. He'd had the love of his life within reach, and he let her slip through his hands.

Susan came home the next day, and they went through their usual routine of her homecoming: dinner and the giving of gifts. She'd always bring him home something from wherever she had been, and he would try to think of something that she wanted but didn't have. She had returned with a newfound love of French cuisine, so she made sure to bring home some herbs and spices.

But there was something different this time. Beyond the spices and the talk of French cuisine, she had something on her mind. She decided to spring it on him at home, while they were sitting at the kitchen island having dinner. She came right out with it.

"I have to tell you something important," she said in her infamous practical tone. "I've met someone."

He nodded slowly, not sure he was hearing her correctly.

"This is in no way your fault, Mark. All this distance between us—it isn't about you. The truth is," she sighed heavily, "my preference is for women. For the first few years of our marriage, I thought that being with such a great guy and having a family would change me." She suddenly looked away, having a hard time admitting her failures. "But of course I was wrong. Nothing can change me."

"I understand," Mark said, although he truly didn't.

She faced him once again. "The marriage has been my cover all these years. I have not wanted the children to guess. But this year, when you suddenly brought up divorce, I realized during counseling that I was not just wasting your time, but I was also wasting mine. When I met a very special woman in France who cared about me, I knew that if I had a chance to fulfill my life and find the kind of love I needed, this was the time to go for it. Our children are grown up and should eventually understand."

"I am surprised," he said in reply, "but not entirely. We have been acting married for quite some time, but not really feeling it. I will always respect our time together. We have raised two wonderful children, and both earned successful careers. There is much to be thankful for." He hoped he sounded sincere; he did mean those things, but the turn of events left him released of a huge burden.

"Yes, we accomplished much together." She leaned over and kissed him briefly, then sat back and exhaled as if to put any bad feelings between them to rest. "Well, you told me you were ready to move on. So now I want to, also. I'm grateful to you for having the courage to bring it up. I apologize for not being the wife you needed; you deserve someone who can be there for you. As for the divorce, I'm sure we can make it amicable all around. I've hired a crew to put my stuff into storage this week, and then following week, I will be going back to France to stay."

"Yes," he agreed. "Amicable will be our mantra. I'll help you with getting your things boxed. Would you like a glass of wine?"

"No, thanks," she answered. "I'm in AA these days. Got to get healthy and live to at least one hundred." She gave him one of her fabulous smiles.

What a turn of events, he thought. He had been ready to tell her he wanted to move on, and instead she was the one with the news. Although he was taken aback, he was very relieved. He had done all the right things; he had tried to make it work. He wondered why he had been so blind as not to realize that she preferred women. Now it made much more sense why she was constantly distancing herself from home and being primarily in the company of women. It dawned on him that Susan hadn't talked about her feelings much to him because of all the emotions she was trying to hide. But then again, he was so caught up in his own feelings of being continually abandoned by her, how could he see around him?

The next day, he made arrangements for the trip to Boston for the reunion. He day dreamed about the possibilities, anxious about what would happen. With his heart at risk, he pinned all his hopes on Melanie.

28

As the end of June approached, the trip to the reunion in Boston loomed. To Melanie, there was a surreal quality about this reunion. It wasn't merely the meeting of old friends. It was more like going back to the roots of her world, a time of youth, love, and excitement. There was something ethereal about it.

Lois was originally skeptical about it, fearing that Melanie was bound for disappointment at this reunion. After all, Melanie had worked hard to achieve perspective over her breakup with Mark. He'd made it clear he wanted no commitment, and he had not contacted her for months. Yet now Melanie wanted to see him. The women met for lunch to talk it over. Lois delivered her latest astrology update.

"I am seeing that there is an opportunity for you to throw off existing circumstances and make a fresh start."

"Really?"

"Yes," Lois replied. "I'm not saying that an opportunity is inevitable. But the possibility is definitely there."

The conversation shifted to Melanie's new grandson, Mark. Melanie couldn't help but wonder about the significance of the name, which she was still having a hard time getting used to. Lois thought it was unrelated to the future, and said that it was probably just the result of random chance. But Melanie still wondered.

Back home, Melanie started to pack the final items she'd need and to put out what Lenny would need for Schneider.

The truth was that Melanie sometimes doubted her decision to divorce Lenny. But in moments of total clarity, she realized that divorce would be best in the long run. *But he had made an amazing epiphany of late. Where did it come from? Was it lasting? Could it be permanent?* In the end, she concluded it was too much of a risk.

The odd thing was that up until now, she had never thought about the long run. Those years that she lived under a bushel, the future didn't exist. At the time, there had been only today and now. There was nothing of life's promise in her thinking. In contrast, she now hoped for a future—if not with Mark, then with someone who would love her for who she was and would be.

As Melanie waited to board her plane for the reunion, she got to thinking about life's odd patterns, its intriguing nuances, and its inevitable consequences. For example, if she hadn't gone to Paris alone, she never would have met Lyle. She was delighted to read his witty and colorful correspondence. Compassionate, sincere, and understanding, he lifted her spirits.

On the flight, she considered the recent changes in her family. Meaghan's brood had settled in. In a few weeks, they could be told about the divorce. Occasionally Lenny would come to her and ask if there was any hope left. She disliked having to answer no, but she didn't want to give him any false hope. As for Eddie, he was thrilled to call Melanie to reveal that he had a girlfriend. There was also a possibility that he would move to Florida, which would put her little family all in one place for once.

On the cab ride to the hotel, she watched all the familiar landmarks pass by. Her mind was steeped in memories of high school. She would be seeing some friends for the first time in over fifty years. So much had happened to her (and she guessed everybody else, too) since those days so long ago. On their graduation day, they had gone out into the world with the words of the valedictorian still ringing in their ears—words of hope, promise, and glory. Well, life did have some of that; but there were a lot of peaks and valleys, too. High school memories would fuel the conversations over the next few days for all those who just couldn't resist attending such a significant reunion. Fifty years was indeed a profoundly significant milestone, and Melanie was curious to see how everyone had turned out.

Melanie checked into the upscale Four Seasons Hotel in downtown Boston, the site of the reunion. Made of glass, stainless steel, and marble, it still exuded a New England flair. She checked in and recognized other reunion people by their name tags and high school pictures on their collars. Some of her classmates were still recognizable. The robust turnout was fabulous; she met and engaged numerous classmates in conversation before she even got to her room to unpack.

Needing a breather, she headed for the hotel lounge, with floor-to-ceiling windows looking out on Boston's Public Garden. It was the perfect atmosphere in which to have coffee and de-compress.

After coffee she returned to the busy lobby. The promise of a good reunion was imminent. It was funny how the personalities and characters of the past seemed to have changed, even while they remained the same—that is except for some extra weight, a plethora of wrinkles, and bald heads. Of course she enjoyed the way most of the men's eyes lingered on her and the compliments she got from both the sincere and the insincere. Some of the conversations with her old group were animated. Short of not spotting Mark anywhere, she was having a good time. She considered that maybe meeting Mark again was not why she had attended the reunion. There were plenty of other interesting people, such as the bouncy and peppy Marge Berger from the cheerleading squad, nerdy Melvin Kaufman from science class, and hunky Rod Elliot, the captain of the football team.

Yet later, as she relaxed in her room, waiting for the evening's program, she felt melancholy. She called Lois to fill her in on everyone, which lifted her spirits. Then there was the primping necessary to make sure that she would look as good as she could.

Similar to most reunions, there was a cocktail party first. She was wearing a black dress, open-toe sandals, and diamond-drop earrings. She meant to look elegant but understated. As she socialized, her mood alternated from bubbly to sadly nostalgic. But one thing was constant: she knew that when she and her old girlfriends perused each other, the question of "plastic surgery or no plastic surgery?" dominated their minds. At one point, she wished she hadn't come.

It was then that she spotted Mark through the crowd. He saw her about the same time. He was wearing his tan, corduroy blazer, black golf shirt, and designer jeans—the sexy way she loved to see him dressed. She stood her ground and waited for him to approach.

She managed to smile when he asked, "Hi. Do you remember me?"

"Of course," Melanie replied, although she didn't remember him from high school at all. "Weren't we in some class together?"

"Yes, it was Spanish. You sat right up front, and I usually sat in the back."

Though he was smiling, the meeting bordered on chilly. The conversation stopped right there, as neither of them knew how to continue. She couldn't shake the feeling that there was something expectant in Mark's eyes, but he never revealed what. Luckily for her, he must have felt her discomfort, because he quickly moved to another group, leaving her to mingle alone.

Melanie lasted throughout the reunion, making all the small talk she could muster. All the while, however, her thoughts were on having lost Mark. When the program was over, she did not mix with the people who had the intention of partying the night away. It was difficult sneaking away. Heading for her room, she was embarrassed that tears were welling in her eyes.

Upon entering her darkened room, she had the sense of a familiar scent. Even before she saw them, she smelled the orchids on the nightstand. They were in a vase with a note, having been brought up by the front desk. She read the note from Mark and burst out crying. The note said, "Meet me in the Governor's Room at midnight." Checking her cell phone, she saw that it was already midnight. *So that's what that look in his eyes was all about!* Would he wait? Ignoring her elevator phobia, she grabbed the first one.

Just outside the Governor's Room, she could hear piano music with a familiar rhythm; it was the Billy Joel song, "Just the Way You Are." She opened the door. The room was dark, illuminated only by candlelight. No one seemed to be there, except two pianists at the piano. There sat Mark, playing the song. Had he forgotten to tell her that he could play? As she approached him, he got up, and the other pianist continued the song. Mark held out his hand to her.

"May I have this dance?"

Melanie was shaky and all but whispered, "Of course." She closed her eyes to savor the moment. They danced as if no one else was on the planet. No one spoke for a while, as neither knew how to begin. Finally, as the song came to an end, Mark gazed into Melanie's eyes and said, "I can't live without you. Now I don't have to, if you still want me."

"Mark!" she exclaimed. "I want to be with you." She paused, and then she added, "I'm now free and single."

He looked at her intently. "You are? So am I."

Wondering if her ears were deceiving her, Melanie asked, "When did this happen?"

Mark smiled and both of them remained quiet for a moment. Finally, he said, "It's a long story that I'll tell you later. What matters is here and now. This is the beginning of our lives as a couple. Whatever it takes, we're in this life together." His next kiss proved what he'd said, and he didn't let her go.

The soothing refrain of another Billy Joel song began from the tinkling piano. They began to dance, the first dance of their future.

She said, "I love the orchids."

"Remember the first time I sent them?"

"Yes," she said. "They look the way we are."

He nodded. "Two orchids, growing in each other's shadow, reaching out to one another."

"For life," she said, the words coming from the depth of her heart.

Epilogue

Dear Melanie,

It was terrific to spend time with you and Mark last week. You're looking great. Living in California suits you well. His boat is fab, and I didn't even get seasick! Thanks for your hospitality.

I wanted you to know how much I've appreciated your friendship over the years. I feel like I've sort of been along for the ride, and I can say that if it's still possible for us to grow at our age, you've certainly come into full bloom.

I know that this growth wasn't easy for you. You risked not being loved in return. I saw you fill your heart with hope, and in doing so, you risked pain. You pursued change, which risked failure. It is what you risked that shows me what you value.

At this time in our lives, when time seems so fleeting, love and friendship are especially sweet.

Yours,

Lois

About the Author

Barbara J. Peters is a successful author and a licensed professional counselor specializing in relationships. In her first book, *The Gift of a Lifetime: Building a Marriage that Lasts*, Barbara lends insight from her years of experience as a couples' counselor. The messages in the book can make the difference between enjoying a second honeymoon or seeking a divorce attorney.

Her second book, *He Said, She Said, I Said*, focuses directly on the issues of communication, trust, forgiveness, intimacy, acceptance, friendship, and love, with a unique approach from three perspectives: the man's, the woman's, and Barbara's (the counselor's).

Barbara received a Bachelor of Arts in sociology from C.W. Post College of Long Island University, a Bachelor of Sciences in nursing from Stony Brook University, and earned a Master of Science in counseling from Georgia State University. She is certified by the National Board of Certified Counselors and is a member of The Licensed Professional Counselors of Georgia.

A Long Island native, Barbara has made Georgia her home for the last twenty-six years; her private counseling practice is in Cumming, Georgia. She is devoted to her family of two grown daughters, four grandchildren, and a Shih Tzu named Gingerlily, who often accompanies her to work.

For more about Barbara and her latest activities,
please visit:
barbarajpeters.com/blog/
www.facebook.com/BarbaraJPeterscom
twitter.com/couplesauthor
www.barbarajpeters.com